The Diamond Master

Jacques Futrelle

THE DIAMOND MASTER

by

JACQUES FUTRELLE

Author of "Elusive Isabel, " "The Thinking Machine, " etc.

1909

CONTENTS

CHAPTER I

THE FIRST DIAMOND

There were thirty or forty personally addressed letters, the daily heritage of the head of a great business establishment; and a plain, yellow-wrapped package about the size of a cigarette-box, some three inches long, two inches wide and one inch deep. It was neatly tied with thin scarlet twine, and innocent of markings except for the superscription in a precise, copperplate hand, and the smudge of the postmark across the ten-cent stamp in the upper right-hand corner. The imprint of the cancellation, faintly decipherable, showed that the package had been mailed at the Madison Square substation at half-past seven o'clock of the previous evening.

Mr. Harry Latham, president and active head of the H. Latham Company, manufacturing jewelers in Fifth Avenue, found the letters and the package on his desk when he entered his private office a few minutes past nine o'clock. The simple fact that the package bore no return address or identifying mark of any sort caused him to pick it up and examine it, after which he shook it inquiringly. Then, with kindling curiosity, he snipped the scarlet thread with a pair of silver scissors, and unfolded the wrappings. Inside was a glazed paper box, such as jewelers use, but still there was no mark, no printing, either on top or bottom.

The cover of the box came off in Mr. Latham's hand, disclosing a bed of white cotton. He removed the downy upper layer, and there— there, nestling against the snowy background, blazed a single splendid diamond, of six, perhaps seven, carats. Myriad colors played in its blue-white depths, sparkling, flashing, dazzling in the subdued light. Mr. Latham drew one long quick breath, and walked over to the window to examine the stone in the full glare of day.

A minute or more passed, a minute of wonder, admiration, allurement, but at last he ventured to lift the diamond from the box. It was perfect, so far as he could see; perfect in cutting and color and depth, prismatic, radiant, bewilderingly gorgeous. Its value? Even he could not offer an opinion—only the appraisement of his expert would be worth listening to on that point. But one thing he knew instantly—in the million-dollar stock of precious stones stored away in the vaults of the H. Latham Company, there was not one to compare with this.

At length, as he stared at it fascinated, he remembered that he didn't know its owner, and for the second time he examined the wrappings, the box inside and out, and finally he lifted out the lower layer of cotton, seeking a fugitive card or mark of some sort. Surely the owner of so valuable a stone would not be so careless as to send it this way, through the mail—unregistered—without some method of identification! Another sharp scrutiny of box and cotton and wrappings left him in deep perplexity.

Then another idea came. One of the letters, of course! The owner of the diamond had sent it this way, perhaps to be set, and had sent instructions under another cover. An absurd, even a reckless thing to do, but ——! And Mr. Latham attacked the heap of letters neatly stacked up in front of him. There were thirty-six of them, but not one even remotely hinted at diamonds. In order to be perfectly sure, Mr. Latham went through his mail a second time. Perhaps the letter of instructions had come addressed to the company, and had gone to the secretary, Mr. Flitcroft.

He arose to summon Mr. Flitcroft from an adjoining room, then changed his mind long enough carefully to replace the diamond in the box and thrust the box into a pigeonhole of his desk. Then he called Mr. Flitcroft in.

"Have you gone through your morning mail? " Mr. Latham inquired of the secretary.

"Yes, " he replied. "I have just finished. "

"Did you happen to come across a letter bearing on—that is, was there a letter to-day, or has there been a letter of instructions as to a single large diamond which was to come, or had come, by mail? "

"No, nothing, " replied Mr. Flitcroft promptly. "The only letter received to-day which referred to diamonds was a notification of a shipment from South Africa. "

Mr. Latham thoughtfully drummed on his desk.

"Well, I'm expecting some such letter, " he explained. "When it comes please call it to my attention. Send my stenographer in. "

Mr. Flitcroft nodded and withdrew; and for an hour or more Mr. Latham was engrossed in the routine of correspondence. There was only an occasional glance at the box in the pigeonhole, and momentary fits of abstraction, to indicate an unabated interest and growing curiosity in the diamond. The last letter was finished, and the stenographer arose to leave.

"Please ask Mr. Czenki to come here, " Mr. Latham directed.

And after a while Mr. Czenki appeared. He was a spare little man, with beady black eyes, bushy brows, and a sinister scar extending from the point of his chin across the right jaw. Mr. Czenki drew a salary of twenty-five thousand dollars a year from the H. Latham Company, and was worth twice that much. He was the diamond expert of the firm; and for five or six years his had been the final word as to quality and value. He had been a laborer in the South African diamond fields—the scar was an assegai thrust—about the time Cecil Rhodes' grip was first felt there; later he was employed as an expert by Barney Barnato at Kimberly, and finally he went to London with Adolph Zeidt. Mr. Latham nodded as he entered, and took the box from the pigeonhole.

"Here's something I'd like you to look at, " he remarked.

Mr. Czenki removed the cover and turned the glittering stone out into his hand. For a minute or more he stood still, examining it, as he turned and twisted it in his fingers, then walked over to a window, adjusted a magnifying glass in his left eye and continued the scrutiny. Mr. Latham swung around in his chair and stared at him intently.

"It's the most perfect blue-white I've ever seen, " the expert announced at last. "I dare say it's the most perfect in the world. "

Mr. Latham arose suddenly and strode over to Mr. Czenki, who was twisting the jewel in his fingers, singling out, dissecting, studying the colorful flashes, measuring the facets with practised eyes, weighing it on his finger-tips, seeking a possible flaw.

"The cutting is very fine, " the expert went on. "Of course I would have to use instruments to tell me if it is mathematically correct; and the weight, I imagine, is—is about six carats, perhaps a fraction more. "

"What's it worth? " asked Mr. Latham. "Approximately, I mean? "

"We know the color is perfect, " explained Mr. Czenki precisely. "If, in addition, the cutting is perfect, and the depth is right, and the weight is six carats or a fraction more, it's worth—in other words, if that is the most perfect specimen in existence, as it seems to be, it's worth whatever you might choose to demand for it—twenty, twenty-five, thirty thousand dollars. With this color, and assuming it to be six carats, even if badly cut, it would be worth ten or twelve thousand. "

Mr. Latham mopped his brow. And this had come by mail, unregistered!

"It would not be possible to say where—where such a stone came from—what country? " Mr. Latham inquired curiously. "What's your opinion? "

The expert shook his head. "If I had to guess I should say Brazil, of course, " he replied; "but that would be merely because the most perfect blue-white diamonds come from Brazil. They are found all over the world—in Africa, Russia, India, China, even in the United States. The simple fact that this color is perfect makes conjecture useless. "

Mr. Latham lapsed into silence, and for a time paced back and forth across his office; Mr. Czenki stood waiting.

"Please get the exact weight, " Mr. Latham requested abruptly. "Also test the cutting. It came into my possession in rather an—an unusual manner, and I'm curious. "

The expert went out. An hour later he returned and placed the white, glazed box on the desk before Mr. Latham.

"The weight is six and three-sixteenths carats, " he stated. "The depth is absolutely perfect according to the diameter of the girdle. The bezel facets are mathematically correct to the minutest fraction—

thirty-three, including the table. The facets on the collet side are equally exact—twenty-five, including the collet, or fifty-eight facets in all. As I said, the color is flawless. In other words, " he continued without hesitation, "I should say, speaking as an expert, that it is the most perfect diamond existing in the world to-day. "

Mr. Latham had been staring at him mutely, and he still sat silent for an instant after Mr. Czenki had finished.

"And its value? " he asked at last.

"Its value! " Mr. Czenki repeated musingly. "You know, Mr. Latham, " he went on suddenly, "there are a hundred experts, commissioned by royalty, scouring the diamond markets of the world for such stones as this. So, if you are looking for a sale and a price, by all means offer it abroad first. " He lifted the sparkling, iridescent jewel from the box again, and gazed at it reflectively. "There is not one stone belonging to the British crown, for instance, which would in any way compare with this. "

"Not even the Koh-i-noor? " Mr. Latham demanded, surprised.

Mr. Czenki shook his head.

"Not even the Koh-i-noor. It is larger, that's all—a fraction more than one hundred and six carats, but it has neither the coloring nor the cutting of this. " There was a pause. "Would it be impertinent if I ask who owns this? "

"I don't know, " replied Mr. Latham slowly. "I don't know; but it isn't ours. Perhaps later I'll be able to—"

"I beg your pardon, " the expert interrupted courteously, and there was a slight expression of surprise on his thin scarred face. "Is that all? "

Mr. Latham nodded absently and Mr. Czenki left the room.

CHAPTER II

TWEEDLEDUM AND TWEEDLEDEE

A little while later, when Mr. Latham started out to luncheon, he thrust the white glazed box into an inside pocket. It had occurred to him that Schultze—Gustave Schultze, the greatest importer of precious stones in America—was usually at the club where he had luncheon, and—

He found Mr. Schultze, a huge blond German, sitting at a table in an alcove, alone, gazing out upon Fifth Avenue in deep abstraction, with perplexed wrinkles about his blue eyes. The German glanced around at Latham quickly as he proceeded to draw out a chair on the opposite side of the table.

"Sid down, Laadham, sid down, " he invited explosively. "I haf yust send der vaiter to der delephone to ask—"

There was a restrained note of excitement in the German's voice, but at the moment it was utterly lost upon Mr. Latham.

"Schultze, you've probably imported more diamonds in the last ten years than any other half-dozen men in the United States, " he interrupted. "I have something here I want you to see. Perhaps, at some time, it may have passed through your hands. "

He placed the glazed box on the table. For an instant the German stared at it with amazed eyes, then one fat hand darted toward it, and he spilled the diamond out on the napkin in his plate. Then he sat gazing as if fascinated by the lambent, darting flashes deep from the blue-white heart.

"Mein Gott, Laadham! " he exclaimed, and with fingers which shook a little he lifted the stone and squinted through it toward the light, with critical eyes. Mr. Latham was leaning forward on the table, waiting, watching, listening.

"Well? " he queried impatiently, at last.

"Laadham, id is der miracle! " Mr. Schultze explained solemnly, with his characteristic, whimsical philosophy. "I haf der dupligade of id, Laadham—der dwin, der liddle brudder. Zee here! "

From an inner pocket he produced a glazed white box, identical with that which Mr. Latham had just set down, then carefully laid the cover aside.

"Look, Laadham, look! "

Mr. Latham looked—and gasped! Here was the counterpart of the mysterious diamond which still lay in Mr. Schultze's outstretched palm.

"Dey are dwins, Laadham, " remarked the German quaintly, finally. "Id came by der mail in dis morning—yust like das, wrapped in paper, but mit no marks, no name, no noddings. Id yust came! "

With his right hand Mr. Latham lifted the duplicate diamond from its cotton bed, and with his left took the other from the German's hand. Then, side by side, he examined them; color, cutting, diameter, depth, all seemed to be the same.

"Dwins, I dell you, " repeated Mr. Schultze stolidly. "Dweedledum und Dweedledee, born of der same mudder und fadder. Laadham, id iss der miracle! Dey are der most beaudiful der world in—yust der pair of dem. "

"Have you made, " Mr. Latham began, and there was an odd, uncertain note in his voice—"Have you made an expert examination? "

"I haf. I measure him, der deepness, der cudding, der facets, und id iss perfect. Und I take my own judgment of a diamond, Laadham, before any man der vorld in but Czenki. "

"And the weight? "

"Prezizely six und d'ree-sixdeendh carads. Dere iss nod more as a difference of a d'irty-second bedween dem. "

Mr. Latham regarded the importer steadily, the while he fought back an absurd, nervous thrill in his voice.

"There isn't that much, Schultze. Their weight is exactly the same. "

For a long time the two men sat staring at each other unseeingly. Finally the German, with a prodigious Teutonic sigh, replaced the diamond from Mr. Latham's right hand in one of the glazed boxes and carefully stowed it away in a cavernous pocket; Mr. Latham mechanically disposed of the other in the same manner.

"Whose are they? " he demanded at length. "Why are they sent to us like this, with no name, no letter of explanation? Until I saw the stone you have I believed this other had been sent to me by some careless fool for setting, perhaps, and that a letter would follow it. I merely brought it here on the chance that it was one of your importations and that you could identify it. But since you have received one under circumstances which seem to be identical, now—" He paused helplessly. "What does it mean? "

Mr. Schultze shrugged his huge shoulders and thoughtfully flicked the ashes from his cigar into the consomme.

"You know, Laadham, " he said slowly, "dey don't pick up diamonds like dose on der streed gorners. I didn't believe dere vas a stone of so bigness in der Unided States whose owner I didn't know id vas. Dose dat are here I haf bring in myself, mostly—dose I did not I haf kept drack of. I don'd know, Laadham, I don'd know. Der longer I lif der more I don'd know. "

The two men completed a scant luncheon in silence.

"Obviously, " remarked Mr. Latham as he laid his napkin aside, "the diamonds were sent to us by the same person; obviously they were sent to us with a purpose; obviously we will, in time, hear from the person who sent them; obviously they were intended to be perfectly matched; so let's see if they are. Come to my office and let Czenki examine the one you have. " He hesitated an instant. "Suppose you let me take it. We'll try a little experiment. "

He carefully placed the jewel which the German handed to him, in an outside pocket, and together they went to his office. Mr. Czenki appeared, in answer to a summons, and Mr. Latham gave him the German's box.

"That's the diamond you examined for me this morning, isn't it? " he inquired.

Mr. Czenki turned it out into his hand and scrutinized it perfunctorily.

"Yes, " he replied after a moment.

"Are you quite certain? " Mr. Latham insisted.

Something in the tone caused Mr. Czenki to raise his beady black eyes questioningly for an instant, after which he walked over to a window and adjusted his magnifying glass again. For a moment or more he stood there, then:

"It's the same stone, " he announced positively.

"Id iss der miracle, Laadham, when Czenki make der mistake! " the German exploded suddenly. "Show him der odder von. "

Mr. Czenki glanced from one to the other with quick, inquisitive glance; then, without a word, Mr. Latham produced the second box and opened it. The expert stared incredulously at the two perfect stones and finally, placing them side by side on a sheet of paper, returned to the window and sat down. Mr. Latham and Mr. Schultze stood beside him, looking on curiously as he turned and twisted the jewels under his powerful glass.

"As a matter of fact, " asked Mr. Latham pointedly at last, "you would not venture to say which of those stones it was you examined this morning, would you? "

"No, " replied Mr. Czenki curtly, "not without weighing them. "

"And if the weight is identical? "

"No, " said Mr. Czenki again. "If the weight is the same there is not the minutest fraction of a difference between them. "

CHAPTER III

THURSDAY AT THREE

Mr. Latham ran through his afternoon mail with feverish haste and found—nothing; Mr. Schultze achieved the same result more ponderously. On the following morning the mail still brought nothing. About eleven o'clock Mr. Latham's desk telephone rang.

"Come to my offiz, " requested Mr. Schultze, in gutteral excitement. "Mein Gott, Laadham, der—come to my offiz, Laadham, und bring der diamond! "

Mr. Latham went. Including himself, there were the heads of the five greatest jewel establishments in America, representing, perhaps, one-tenth of the diamond trade of the country, in Mr. Schultze's office. He found the other four gathered around a small table, and on this table—Mr. Latham gasped as he looked—lay four replicas of the mysterious diamond in his pocket.

"Pud id down here, Laadham, " directed Mr. Schultze. "Dey're all dwins alike—Dweedeldums und Dweedledeeses. "

Mr. Latham silently placed the fifth diamond on the table, and for a minute or more the five men stood still and gazed, first at the diamonds, then at one another, and then again at the diamonds. Mr. Solomon, the crisply spoken head of Solomon, Berger and Company, broke the silence.

"These all came yesterday morning by mail, one to each of us just as the one came to you, " he informed Mr. Latham. "Mr. Harris here, of Harris and Blacklock, learned that I had received such a stone, and brought the one he had received for comparison. We made some inquiries together and found that a duplicate had been received by Mr. Stoddard, of Hall-Stoddard-Higginson. The three of us came here to see if Mr. Schultze could give us any information, and he telephoned for you. "

Mr. Latham listened blankly.

"It's positively beyond belief, " he burst out. "What—what does it mean? "

"Id means, " the German importer answered philosophically, "dat if diamonds like dese keep popping up like dis, dat in anoder d'ree months dey vill nod be vorth more as five cents a bucketful. "

The truth of the observation came to the four others simultaneously. Hitherto there had been only the sense of wonder and admiration; now came the definite knowledge that diamonds, even of such great size and beauty as these, would grow cheap if they were to be picked out of the void; and realization of this astonishing possibility brought five shrewd business brains to a unit of investigation. First it was necessary to find how many other jewelers had received duplicates; then it was necessary to find whence they came. A plan was adopted, and an investigation ordered to begin at once.

"Dere iss someding back of id, of course, " declared Mr. Schultze. "Vas iss? Dey are nod being send for our healdh! "

During the next six days half a score of private detectives were at work on the mystery, with the slender clews at hand. They scanned hotel registers, quizzed paper-box manufacturers, pestered stamp clerks, bedeviled postal officials, and the sum total of their knowledge was negative, save in the fact that they established beyond question that only these five men had received the diamonds.

And meanwhile the heads of the five greatest jewel houses in New York were assiduous in their search for that copperplate superscription in their daily mail. On the morning of the eighth day it came. Mr. Latham was nervously shuffling his unopened personal correspondence when he came upon it—a formal white square envelope, directed by that same copperplate hand which had directed the boxes. He dropped into his chair, and opened the envelope with eager fingers. Inside was this letter:

MY DEAR SIR:

One week ago I took the liberty of sending to you, and to each of four other leading jewelers of this city whose names you know, a single large diamond of rare cutting and color. Please accept this as a gift from me, and be good enough to convey my compliments to the other four gentlemen, and assure them that theirs, too, were gifts.

The Diamond Master

Believe me, I had no intention of making a mystery of this. It was necessary definitely to attract your attention, and I could conceive of no more certain way than in this manner. In return for the value of the jewels I shall ask that you and the four others concerned give me an audience in your office on Thursday afternoon next at three o'clock; that you make known this request to the others; and that three experts whose judgment you will all accept shall meet with us.

I believe you will appreciate the necessity of secrecy in this matter, for the present at least. Respectfully,

E. VAN CORTLANDT WYNNE

They were on hand promptly, all of them—Mr. Latham, Mr. Schultze, Mr. Solomon, Mr. Stoddard and Mr. Harris. The experts agreed upon were the unemotional Mr. Czenki, Mr. Cawthorne, an Englishman in the employ of Solomon, Berger and Company, and Mr. Schultze, who gravely admitted that he was the first expert in the land, after Mr. Czenki, and whose opinion of himself was unanimously accepted by the others. The meeting place was the directors' room of the H. Latham Company.

At one minute of three o'clock a clerk entered with a card, and handed it to Mr. Latham.

"'Mr. E. van Cortlandt Wynne, '" Mr. Latham read aloud, and every man in the room moved a little in his chair. Then: "Show him in here, please. "

"Now, gendlemens, " observed Mr. Schultze sententiously, "ve shall zee vat ve shall zee. "

The clerk went out and a moment later Mr. Wynne appeared. He was tall and rather slender, alert of eyes, graceful of person; perfectly self-possessed and sure of himself, yet without one trace of egotism in manner or appearance—a fair type of the brisk, courteous young business man of New York. He wore a tweed suit, and in his left hand carried a small sole-leather grip. For an instant he stood, framed by the doorway, meeting the sharp scrutiny of the assembled jewelers with a frank smile. For a little time no one spoke—merely gazed—and finally:

"Mr. Latham? " queried Mr. Wynne, looking from one to the other.

Mr. Latham came to his feet with a sudden realization of his responsibilities as a temporary host, and introductions followed. Mr. Wynne passed along on one side of the table, shaking hands with each man in turn until he came to Mr. Czenki. Mr. Latham introduced them.

"Mr. Czenki, " repeated Mr. Wynne, and he allowed his eyes to rest frankly upon the expert for a moment. "Your name has been repeated to me so often that I almost feel as if I knew you. "

Mr. Czenki bowed without speaking.

"I am assuming that this is the Mr. Czenki who was associated with Mr. Barnato and Mr. Zeidt? " the young man went on.

"That is correct, yes, " replied the expert.

"And I believe, too, that you once did some special work for Professor Henri Moissan in Paris? "

Mr. Czenki's black eyes seemed to be searching the other's face for an instant, and then he nodded affirmatively.

"I made some tests for him, yes, " he volunteered.

Mr. Wynne passed on along the other side of the long table, and stopped at the end. Mr. Latham was at his right, Mr. Schultze at his left, and Mr. Czenki sat at the far end, facing him. The small sole-leather grip was on the floor at Mr. Wynne's feet. For a moment he permitted himself to enjoy the varying expressions of interest on the faces around the table.

"Gentlemen, " he began, then, "you all, probably, have seen my letter to Mr. Latham, or at least you are aware of its contents, so you understand that the diamonds which were mailed to you are your property. I am not a eleemosynary institution for the relief of diamond merchants, " and he smiled a little, "for the gifts are preliminary to a plain business proposition—a method of concentrating your attention, and, in themselves, part payment, if I may say it, for any worry or inconvenience which followed upon their appearance. There are only five of them in the world, they are precisely alike, and they are yours. I beg of you to accept them with my compliments. "

Mr. Schultze tilted his chair back a little, the better to study the young man's countenance.

"I am going to make some remarkable statements, " the young man continued, "but each of those statements is capable of demonstration here and now. Don't hesitate to interrupt if there is a question in your mind, because everything I shall say is vital to each of you as bearing on the utter destruction of the world's traffic in diamonds. It is coming, gentlemen, it is coming, just as inevitably as that night follows day, unless you stop it. You can stop it by concerted action, in a manner which I shall explain later. "

He paused and glanced along the table. Only the face of Mr. Czenki was impassive.

"Since the opening of the fields in South Africa, " Mr. Wynne resumed quietly, "something like five hundred million dollars' worth of diamonds have been found there; and we'll say arbitrarily that all the other diamond fields of the world, including Brazil and Australia, have produced another five hundred million dollars' worth —in other words, since about 1868 a billion dollars' worth of diamonds has been placed upon the market. Gentlemen, that represents millions and millions of carats—forty, fifty, sixty million carats in the rough, say. Please bear those figures in mind a moment.

"Now, suddenly, and as yet secretly, the diamond output of the world has been increased fiftyfold—that is, gentlemen, within the year I can place another billion dollars' worth of diamonds, at the prices that hold now, in the open market; and within still another year I can place still another billion in the market; and on and on indefinitely. To put it differently, I have found the unlimited supply. "

"Mein Gott, vere iss id? " demanded the German breathlessly.

Heedless of the question, Mr. Wynne leaned forward on the table, and gazed with half-closed eyes into the faces before him. Incredulity was the predominant expression, and coupled with that was amazement. Mr. Harris, with quite another emotion displaying itself on his face, pushed back his chair as if to rise; a slight wrinkle in his brow was all the evidence of interest displayed by Mr. Czenki.

"I am not crazy, gentlemen, " Mr. Wynne went on after a moment, and the perfectly normal voice seemed to reassure Mr. Harris, for he sat still. "The diamonds are now in existence, untold millions of dollars' worth of them—but there is the tedious work of cutting. They're in existence, packed away as you pack potatoes—I thrust my two hands into a bag and bring them out full of stones as perfect as the ones I sent you. "

He straightened up again and the deep earnestness of his face relaxed a little.

"I believe you said, Mr. Wynne, that you could prove any assertion you might make, here and now? " suggested Mr. Latham coldly. "It occurs to me that such extraordinary statements as these demand immediate proof. "

Mr. Wynne turned and smiled at him.

"You are quite right, " he agreed; and then, to all of them: "It's hardly necessary to dwell upon the value of colored diamonds—the rarest and most precious of all—the perfect rose-color, the perfect blue and the perfect green. " He drew a small, glazed white box from his pocket and opened it. "Please be good enough to look at this, Mr. Czenki. "

He spun a rosily glittering object some three-quarters of an inch in diameter, along the table toward Mr. Czenki. It flamed and flashed as it rolled, with that deep iridescent blaze which left no doubt of what it was. Every man at the table arose and crowded about Mr. Czenki, who held a flamelike sphere in his outstretched palm for their inspection. There was a tense, breathless instant.

"It's a diamond! " remarked Mr. Czenki, as if he himself had doubted it. "A deep rose-color, cut as a perfect sphere. "

"It's worth half a million dollars if it's worth a cent! " exclaimed Mr. Solomon almost fiercely.

"And this, please. "

Mr. Wynne, from the other end of the table, spun another glittering sphere toward them—this as brilliantly, softly green as the verdure of early spring, prismatic, gleaming, radiant. Mr. Czenki's beady eyes snapped as he caught it and held it out for the others to see, and some strange emotion within caused him to close his teeth savagely.

"And this! " said Mr. Wynne again.

And a third sphere rolled along the table. This was blue—elusively blue as a moonlit sky. Its rounded sides caught the light from the windows and sparkled it back.

And now the three jewels lay side by side in Mr. Czenki's open hand, the while the five greatest diamond merchants of the United States glutted their eyes upon them. Mr. Latham's face went deathly white from sheer excitement, the German's violently red from the same emotion, and the others—there was amazement, admiration, awe in them. Mr. Czenki's countenance was again impassive.

CHAPTER IV

THE UNLIMITED SUPPLY

"If you will all be seated again, please? " requested Mr. Wynne, who still stood, cool and self-certain, at the end of the table.

The sound of his voice brought a returning calm to the others, and they resumed their seats—all save Mr. Cawthorne, who walked over to a window with the three spheres in his hand and stood there examining them under his glass.

"You gentlemen know, of course, the natural shape of the diamond in the rough? " Mr. Wynne resumed questioningly. "Here are a dozen specimens which may interest you—the octahedron, the rhombic dodecahedron, the triakisoctahedron and the hexakisoctahedron. " He spread them along the table with a sweeping gesture of his hand, colorless, inert pebbles, ranging in size from a pea to a peanut. "And now, you ask, where do they come from? "

The others nodded unanimously.

"I'll have to state a fact that you all know, as part answer to that question, " replied Mr. Wynne. "A perfect diamond is a perfect diamond, no matter where it comes from—Africa, Brazil, India or New Jersey. There is not the slightest variation in value if the stone is perfect. That being true, it is a matter of no concern to you, as dealers, where these come from—sufficient it is that they are here, and, being here, they bring home to you the necessity of concerted action to uphold the diamond as a thing of value. "

"You said der vorld's oudpud had been increased fiftyfold? " suggested Mr. Schultze. "Do ve understand you prove him by dese? "

The young man smiled slightly and drew a leather packet from an inner pocket. He stripped it of several rubber bands, and then turned to Mr. Czenki again.

"Mr. Czenki, I have been told that a few years ago you had an opportunity of examining the Koh-i-noor. Is that correct? "

"Yes. "

"I believe the Koh-i-noor was temporarily removed from its setting, and that you were one of three experts to whom was intrusted the task of selecting four stones of the identical coloring to be set alongside it? "

"That is correct, " Mr. Czenki agreed.

"You held the Koh-i-noor in your hand, and you would be able to identify it? "

"I would be able to identify it, " said Mr. Cawthorne positively.

He had turned at the window quickly; it was the first time he had spoken. Mr. Wynne walked around the table to Mr. Czenki, and Mr. Cawthorne approached them.

"Suppose, then, you gentlemen examine this together, " suggested Mr. Wynne.

He lifted a great glittering jewel from the leather packet and held it aloft that all might see. Then he carefully placed it on the table in front of the experts; the others came to their feet and stood gazing as if fascinated.

"By Jove! " exclaimed Mr. Cawthorne.

For a minute or more the two experts studied the huge diamond—one hundred and six carats and a fraction—beneath their glasses, and finally Mr. Cawthorne picked it up and led the way toward the window. Mr. Czenki and the German followed him.

"Gentlemen, " and Mr. Cawthorne now turned sharply to face the others, "this is the Koh-i-noor! Mr. Czenki didn't mention it, but I was one of the three experts who had opportunity to examine the Koh-i-noor. This is the Koh-i-noor! "

Startled, questioning eyes were turned upon Mr. Wynne; he was smiling. There was a question in his face as he regarded Mr. Czenki.

"It is either the Koh-i-noor or an exact duplicate, " said Mr. Czenki.

"It is the Koh-i-noor, " repeated Mr. Cawthorne doggedly.

"Id seems to me, " interposed Mr. Schultze, "dat if der Koh-i-noor vas missing somebody would haf heard, ain'd id? I haf nod heard. Mr. Czenki made a misdake der oder day—maybe you make id to-day? "

"You have made a mistake, I assure you, Mr. Cawthorne, " remarked Mr. Wynne quietly. "You identify that as the Koh-i-noor, of course, by a slight inaccuracy in one of the facets adjoining the collet. That inaccuracy is known to every diamond expert—the mistake you make is a compliment to that as a replica. "

He resumed his position at the end of the table, and Mr. Schultze sat beside him. Amazement was a thing of the past, as far as he was concerned. Mr. Czenki dropped into his chair again.

"And now, Mr. Czenki, speaking as an expert, what would you say was the most perfect diamond the world? " asked Mr. Wynne.

"The five blue-white stones you mailed to these gentlemen, " replied the expert without hesitation.

"Perhaps I should have specified the most perfect diamond known to the world at large, " Mr. Wynne added smilingly.

"The Regent. "

Again Mr. Cawthorne looked around, with bewilderment in his eyes. The others nodded their approval of Mr. Czenki's opinion.

"The Regent, yes, " Mr. Wynne agreed; "one hundred and thirty-six and three-quarter carats, cut as a brilliant, worn by Napoleon in his sword-hilt, now in the Louvre at Paris, the property of the French Government—valued at two and a half million dollars. " His hand disappeared into the leather packet again; poised on his finger-tips, when he withdrew them, was another huge jewel. He dropped it into Mr. Schultze's hand. "There is further proof that the diamond output has increased fiftyfold. "

Mr. Schultze seemed dazed as he turned and twisted the diamond in his hand. After a moment he passed it on down the table without a word.

"A duplicate also, " and Mr. Wynne glanced at Mr. Cawthorne. "It is reasonably certain that you would have heard of that if it had disappeared from the Louvre. " He turned to Mr. Schultze again. "I may add that this fiftyfold increase in output is not confined to small stones, " he went on tauntingly. "They are of all sizes and values. For instance? "

He lifted still another jewel from the packet and held it aloft for an instant.

"The Orloff! " gasped Mr. Solomon.

"No, " the young man corrected; "this, too, is a duplicate. The original is in the Russian sceptre. This is a replica—color, weight and cutting being identical—one hundred and ninety-three carats, nearly as large as a pigeon's egg. "

Again Mr. Wynne glanced along the table. Suddenly the frank amazement had vanished from the faces of these men, and he found only the tense interest of an audience watching a clever juggler. For a time Mr. Schultze studied the Orloff duplicate, then passed it along to the experts.

"Der grand Cullinan diamond weighs only two or d'ree pounds, " he questioned in a tone of deep resignation. "Maybe you haf him in der backage, alretty? "

"Not yet, " replied Mr. Wynne, "but I may possibly get that on my next trip out. Who knows? "

There was a long, tense silence. Mechanically Mr. Czenki placed the three spheres and the replicas in an orderly little row on the table in front of him and the uncut stones beside them—six, seven, eight million dollars' worth of diamonds.

"Gentlemen, are you convinced? " demanded Mr. Wynne suddenly. "Is there one lingering doubt in any mind here as to the tremendous find which makes the production of all those possible? "

"Id iss der miracle, Mr. Vynne, " admitted the German gravely, after a little pause. "Dere iss someding before us as nefer vas in der vorld. I am gonvinced! "

"Up to this moment, gentlemen, the De Beers Syndicate has controlled the diamond market, " Mr. Wynne announced, "but now, from this moment, I control it. I hold it there, in the palm of my hand, with the unlimited supply back of me. I am offering you an opportunity to prevent the annihilation of the market. It rests with you. If I turn loose a billion dollars' worth of diamonds within the year you are ruined—all of you. You know that—it's hardly necessary to tell you. And, gentlemen, I don't care to do it. "

"What is your proposition? " queried Mr. Latham quietly. His face was ghastly white; haggard lines, limned by amazement and realization, were marked clearly on it. "What is your proposition? " he repeated.

"Wait a minute, " interposed Mr. Solomon protestingly, and he turned to the young man. "The Syndicate controls the market by force of a reserve stock of ten or fifteen million dollars. Do we understand that you have more than these ready for market now? "

Mr. Wynne stooped and lifted the small sole-leather grip which had been unheeded on the floor. He unfastened the catch and turned the bag upside down upon the table. When he raised it again the assembled jewelers gazed upon a spectacle unknown and undreamed of in the history of the world—a great, glittering heap of diamonds, flashing, colorful, prismatic, radiant, bedazzling. They rattled like pebbles upon the mahogany table as they slipped and slid one against another, and then, at rest, resolved themselves into a steady, multi-colored blaze which was almost blinding.

"Now, gentlemen, on the table before you there are about thirty million dollars' worth of diamonds, " Mr. Wynne announced calmly. "They are all perfect, every one of them; and they're mine. I know where they come from; you can't find out. It's none of your business. Are you satisfied now? "

Mr. Latham looked, looked until his eyes seemed bursting from his head, and then, with an inarticulate little cry, fell forward on the table with his face on his arms. The German importer came to his feet with one vast Teutonic oath, then sat down again; Mr. Solomon plunged his hand into the blazing heap and laughed senselessly. The others were silent, stunned, overcome. Mr. Wynne walked around the table and replaced the spheres and replicas in his pocket, after which he resumed his former position.

"I have stated my case, gentlemen, " he continued quietly, very quietly. "Now for my proposition. Briefly it is this: For a consideration I will destroy the unlimited supply. I will bind myself to secrecy, as you must; I will guarantee that no stone from the same source is ever offered in the market or privately, while you gentlemen, " and his manner was emphatically deliberate, "purchase from me at one-half the carat price you now pay one hundred million dollars' worth of diamonds! "

He paused. There was not a sound; no one moved.

"You may put them on the market as you may agree, slowly, thus preventing any material fluctuation in value, " he went on. "How to hold this tremendous reserve secretly and still permit the operation of the other diamond mines of the world is the great problem you will have to face. "

He leaned over, picked up a handful from the heap and replaced them in the leather bag. The others he swept off into it, then snapped the lock.

"I will give you one week to decide what you will do, " he said in conclusion. "If you accept the proposition, then six weeks from next Thursday at three o'clock I shall expect a cash payment of ten million dollars for a portion of the stones now cut and ready; within a year all the diamonds will have been delivered and the transaction must be closed. " He hesitated an instant. "I'm sorry, gentlemen, if the terms seem hard, but I think, after consideration, you will agree that I have done you a favor by coming to you instead of going into the market and destroying it. I will call next Thursday at three for your answer. That is all. Good day! "

The door opened and closed behind him. A minute, two minutes, three minutes passed and no one spoke. At last the German came to his feet slowly with a sigh.

"Anyhow, gendlemens, " he remarked, "dat young man has a hell of a lod of diamonds, ain'd id? "

CHAPTER V

THE ASTUTE MR. BIRNES

It was a few minutes past four o'clock when Mr. Wynne strode through the immense retail sales department of the H. Latham Company, and a uniformed page held open the front door for him to pass out. Once on the sidewalk the self-styled diamond master of the world paused long enough to pull on his gloves, carelessly chucking the small sole-leather grip with its twenty-odd million dollars' worth of precious stones under one arm; then he turned up Fifth Avenue toward Thirty-fourth Street. A sneak thief brushed past him, appraised him with one furtive glance, then went his way, seeking quarry more promising.

Simultaneously with Mr. Wynne's appearance three men whose watchful eyes had been fastened on the doorway of the H. Latham Company for something more than an hour stirred. One of them— Frank Claflin—was directly across the street, strolling along idly, the most purposeless of all in the hurrying, well-dressed throng; another—Steve Birnes, chief of the Birnes Detective Agency— appeared from the hallway of a building adjoining the H. Latham Company, and moved along behind Mr. Wynne, some thirty feet in the rear; the third—Jerry Malone—was half a block away, up Fifth Avenue, coming slowly toward them.

Mr. Birnes adjusted his pace to that of Mr. Wynne, step for step, and then, seeming assured of his safety from any chance glance, ostentatiously mopped his face with a handkerchief, flirting it a little to the left as he replaced it in his pocket. Claflin, across the street, understood from that that he was to go on up Fifth Avenue to Thirty-fourth Street, the next intersection, and turn west to board any crosstown car which Mr. Wynne might possibly take; and a cabby, who had been sitting motionless on his box down the street, understood from it that he was to move slowly along behind Mr. Birnes, and be prepared for an emergency.

Half-way between Thirty-third and Thirty-fourth Streets, Jerry Malone approached and passed Mr. Wynne without so much as a glance at him, and went on toward his chief.

"Drop in behind here, " Mr. Birnes remarked crisply to Malone, without looking around. "I'll walk on ahead and turn east in Thirty-fourth Street to nail him if he swings a car. Claflin's got him going west. "

Mr. Wynne was perhaps some twenty feet from the corner of Thirty-fourth Street and Fifth Avenue when Mr. Birnes passed him. His glance lingered on the broad back of the chief reflectively as he swung by and turned into the cross street, after a quick, business-like glance at an approaching car. Then Mr. Wynne smiled. He paused on the edge of the curb long enough for an automobile to pass, then went on across Thirty-fourth Street to the uptown side and, turning flatly, looked Mr. Birnes over pensively, after which he leaned up against an electric-light pole and scribbled something on an envelope.

A closed cab came wriggling and squirming up Fifth Avenue. As it reached the middle of Thirty-fourth Street Mr. Wynne raised his hand, and the cab drew up beside him. He said something to the driver, opened the door and stepped in. Mr. Birnes smiled confidently. So that was it, eh? He, too, crossed Thirty-fourth Street and lifted his hand. The cab which had been drifting along behind him immediately came up.

"Now, Jimmy, get on the job, " instructed Mr. Birnes, as he stepped in. "Keep that chap in sight and when he stops you stop. "

Mr. Wynne's cab jogged along comfortably up the avenue, twisting and winding a path between the other vehicles, the while Mr. Birnes regarded it with thoughtful gaze. Its number dangled on a white board in the rear; Mr. Birnes just happened to note it.

"Grand Central Station, I'll bet a hat, " he mused.

But the closed cab didn't turn into Forty-second Street; it went past, then on past Delmonico's, past the Cathedral, past the Plaza, at Fifty-ninth Street, and still on uptown. It was not hurrying— it merely moved steadily; but once free of the snarl which culminates at the Fifty-ninth Street entrance to Central Park, its speed was increased a little. Past Sixty-fourth Street, Sixty-fifth, Sixty-sixth, and at Sixty-seventh it slowed up and halted at the sidewalk on the far side.

"Stop in front of a door, Jimmy, " directed the detective hastily.

Jimmy obeyed gracefully, and Mr. Birnes stepped out, hardly half a block behind the closed cab. He went through an elaborate pretense of paying Jimmy, the while he regarded Mr. Wynne, who had also alighted and was paying the driver. The small sole-leather grip was on the ground between his feet as he ransacked his pocketbook. A settlement was reached, the cabby nodded, touched his horse with his whip and continued to jog on up Fifth Avenue.

"Now, he didn't order that chap to come back or he wouldn't have paid him, " the detective reasoned. "Therefore he's close to where he is going. "

But Mr. Wynne seemed in no hurry; instead he stood still for a minute gazing after the retreating vehicle, which fact made it necessary for Mr. Birnes to start a dispute with Jimmy as to just how much the fare should be. They played the scene admirably; had Mr. Wynne been listening he might even have heard part of the vigorous argument. Whether he listened or not he turned and gazed straight at Mr. Birnes until, finally, the detective recognized the necessity of getting out of sight.

With a final explosion he handed a bill to Jimmy and turned to go up the steps of the house. He had no business there, but he must do something.

Jimmy turned the cab short and went rattling away down Fifth Avenue to await orders in the lee of a corner a block or so away. And, meanwhile, as Mr. Wynne still stood on the corner, Mr. Birnes had to go on up the steps. But as he placed his foot on the third step he knew—though he had not looked, apparently, yet he knew—that Mr. Wynne had raised his hand, and that in that hand was a small white envelope. And further, he knew that Mr. Wynne was gazing directly at him.

Now that was odd. Slowly it began to dawn upon the detective that Mr. Wynne was trying to attract his attention. If he heeded the signal—evidently it was intended as such—it would be a confession that he was following Mr. Wynne, and realizing this he took two more steps up. Mr. Wynne waved the envelope again, after which he folded it across twice and thrust it into a crevice of a water-plug beside him. Then he turned east along Sixty-seventh Street and disappeared.

The detective had seen the performance, all of it, and he was perplexed. It was wholly unprecedented. However, the first thing to do now was to keep Mr. Wynne in sight, so he came down the steps and walked rapidly on to Sixty-seventh Street, pausing to peer around the corner before he turned. Mr. Wynne was idling along, half a block away, without the slightest apparent interest in what was happening behind. Inevitably Mr. Birnes' eyes were drawn to the water-plug across the street. A tag end of white paper gleamed tantalizingly. Now what the deuce did it mean?

Being only human, Mr. Birnes went across the street and got the paper. It was an envelope. As he unfolded it and gazed at the address, written in pencil, his mouth opened in undignified astonishment. It was addressed to him—Steve Birnes, Chief of the Birnes Detective Agency. Mr. Wynne had still not looked back, so the detective trailed along behind, opening the envelope as he walked. A note inside ran briefly:

My address is No. — — East Thirty-seventh Street. If it is necessary for you to see me please call there about six o'clock this afternoon. E. VAN CORTLANDT WYNNE

Now here was, perhaps, as savory a kettle of fish as Mr. Birnes had ever stumbled upon. It is difficult to imagine a more embarrassing situation for the professional sleuth than to find himself suddenly taken into the confidence of the person he is shadowing. But was he being taken into Mr. Wynne's confidence? Ah! That was the question! Admitting that Mr. Wynne knew who he was, and admitting that he knew he was being followed, was not this apparent frankness an attempt to throw him off the scent? He would see, would Mr. Birnes.

He quickened his pace a little, then slowed up instantly, because Mr. Wynne had stopped on the corner of Madison Avenue, and as a downtown car came rushing along he stepped out to board it. Mr. Birnes scuttled across the street, and by a dexterous jump swung on the car as it fled past. Mr. Wynne had gone forward and was taking a seat; Mr. Birnes remained on the back platform, sheltered by the accommodating bulk of a fat man, and flattered himself that Mr. Wynne had not seen him. By peering over a huge shoulder the detective was still able to watch Mr. Wynne.

He saw him pay his fare, and then he saw him place the small sole-leather grip on his knees and unfasten the catch. Not knowing what was in that grip Mr. Birnes was curious to see what came out of it. Nothing came out of it—it was empty! There was no question of this, for Mr. Wynne opened it wide and turned it upside down to shake it out. It didn't mean anything in particular to Mr. Birnes, the fact that the grip was empty, so he didn't get excited about it.

Mr. Wynne left the car at Thirty-fourth Street, the south end of the Park Avenue tunnel, by the front door, and the detective stepped off the rear end. Mr. Wynne brushed past him as he went up the stairs, and as he did so he smiled a little—a very little. He walked on up Park Avenue to Thirty-seventh Street, turned in there and entered a house about the middle of the block, with a latch-key. The detective glanced at the number of the house, and felt aggrieved—it was the number that was written in the note! And Mr. Wynne had entered with a key! Which meant, in all probability, that he did live there, as he had said!

But why did he take that useless cab ride up Fifth Avenue? If he had no objection to any one knowing his address, why did he go so far out of his way? Mr. Birnes couldn't say. As he pondered these questions he saw a maid-servant come out of a house adjoining that which Mr. Wynne had entered, an he went up boldly to question her.

Did a Mr. Wynne live next door? Yes. How long had he lived there? Five or six months. Did he own the house? No. The people who owned the house had gone to Europe for a year and had rented it furnished. No, Mr. Wynne didn't have a family. He lived there alone except for two servants, a cook and a housemaid. She had never noticed anything unusual about Mr. Wynne, or the servants, or the house. Yes, he went out every day, downtown to business. No, she didn't know what his business was, but she had an idea that he was a broker. That was all.

From a near-by telephone booth the detective detailed Claflin and Malone, who had returned to the office, to keep a sharp watch on the house, after which he walked on to Fifth Avenue, and down Fifth Avenue to the establishment of the H. Latham Company. Mr. Latham would see him—yes. In fact, Mr. Latham, harried by the events of the past two hours, bewildered by a hundred-million-dollar diamond deal which had been thrust down his throat gracefully, but none the less certainly, and ridden by the keenest curiosity, was delighted to see Mr. Birnes.

"I've got his house address all right, " Mr. Birne boasted, in the beginning. Of course it was against the ethics of the profession to tell how he got it.

"Progress already, " commented Mr. Latham with keen interest. "That's good. "

Then the detective detailed the information he had received from the maid, adding thereto divers and sundry conclusions of his own.

Mr. Latham marveled exceedingly.

"He tried to shake us all right when he went out, " Mr. Birnes went on to explain, "but the trap was set and there was no escape. "

With certain minor omissions he told of the cab ride to Sixty-seventh Street, the trip across to a downtown car, and, as a matter of convincing circumstantial detail, added the incident of the empty gripsack.

"Empty? " repeated Mr. Latham, startled. "Empty, did you say? "

"Empty as a bass drum, " the detective assured him complacently. "He turned it upside down and shook it. "

"Then what became of them? " demanded Mr. Latham.

"Became of what? "

"The diamonds, man—what became of the diamonds? "

"You didn't mention any diamonds to me except those five the other day, " the detective reminded him coldly. "Your instructions were to find out all about this man—who he is, what he does, where he goes, and the rest. This is my preliminary report. You didn't mention diamonds. "

"I didn't know he would have them, " Mr. Latham exploded irascibly. "That empty gripsack, man—when he left here he carried millions—I mean a great quantity of diamonds in it. "

"A great quantity of —, " the detective began; and then he sat up straight in his chair and stared at Mr. Latham in bewilderment.

"If the gripsack was empty when he was on the car, " Mr. Latham rushed on excitedly, "then don't you see that he got rid of the diamonds somehow from the time he left here until you saw that the gripsack was empty? How did he get rid of them? Where does he keep them? And where does he get them? "

Mr. Birnes closed his teeth grimly and his eyes snapped. Now he knew why Mr. Wynne had taken that useless cab ride up Fifth Avenue. It was to enable him to get rid of the diamonds! There was an accomplice—in detective parlance the second person is always an accomplice—in that closed cab! It had all been prearranged; Mr. Wynne had deliberately made a monkey of him—Steven Birnes! Reluctantly the detective permitted himself to remember that he didn't know whether there was anybody in that cab or not when Mr. Wynne entered it, and—and—! Then he remembered that he did know one thing—the number of the cab!

He arose abruptly, with the light of a great determination in his face.

"Whose diamonds were they? " he demanded.

"They were his, as far as we know, " replied Mr. Latham.

"How much were they worth? "

Mr. Latham looked him over thoughtfully.

"I am not at liberty to tell you that, Mr. Birnes, " he said at last. "There are a great number of them, and they are worth—they are worth a large sum of money. And they are all unset. That's enough for you to know, I think. "

It seemed to be quite enough for Mr. Birnes to know.

"It may be that I will have something further to report this evening, " he told Mr. Latham. "If not, I'll see you to-morrow, here. "

He went out. Ten minutes later he was talking to a friend in police headquarters, over the telephone. The records there showed that the license for the particular cab he had followed had been issued to one

William Johns. He was usually to be found around the cabstand in Madison Square, and lived in Charlton Street.

CHAPTER VI

THE MYSTERIOUS WOMAN

Mr. Birnes' busy heels fairly spurned the pavements of Fifth Avenue as he started toward Madison Square. Here was a long line of cabs drawn up beside the curb, some twenty or thirty in all. The fifth from the end bore the number he sought—Mr. Birnes chuckled; and there, alongside it, stood William Johns, swapping Billingsgate with the driver of a hansom, the while he kept one eye open for a prospective fare. It was too easy! Mr. Birnes paused long enough to congratulate himself upon his marvelous acumen, and then he approached the driver.

"You are William Johns? " he accused him sharply.

"That's me, Cap, " the cabby answered readily.

"A few minutes past four o'clock this afternoon you went up Fifth Avenue, and stopped at the corner of Thirty-fourth Street to pick up a fare—a young man. "

"Yep. "

"You drove him to the corner of Sixty-seventh Street and Fifth Avenue, " the detective went on just to forestall possible denials. "He got out there, paid you, and you went on up Fifth Avenue. "

"Far be it from me to deceive you, Cap, " responded the cabby with irritating levity. "I done that same. "

"Who was that man? " demanded Mr. Birnes coldly.

"Search me! I never seen him before. "

The detective regarded the cabby with accusing eyes. Then, quite casually, he flipped open his coat and Johns caught a glimpse of a silver shield. It might only have been accident, of course, still—

"Now, Johns, who was the man in the cab when you stopped to pick up the second man at Thirty-fourth Street? "

"Wrong, Cap, " and the cabby grinned. "There wasn't any man. "

"Don't attempt to deny—"

"No man, Cap. It was a woman. "

"A woman! " the detective repeated. "A woman! "

"Sure thing—a woman, a regular woman. And, Cap, she was a pippin, a peachorino, a beauty bright, " he added, gratuitously.

Mr. Birnes stared thoughtfully across the street for a little while. So there was a woman in it! Mr. Wynne had transferred the contents of the gripsack to her, in a cab, on a crowded thoroughfare, right under his nose!

"I was a little farther down the line there, " Johns went on to explain. "About a quarter of four o'clock, I guess, she came along. She got in, after telling me to drive slowly up Fifth Avenue so I would pass Thirty-fourth Street five minutes or so after four o'clock. If a young man with a gripsack hailed me at the corner I was to stop and let him get in; then I was to go on up Fifth Avenue. If I wasn't stopped I was to drive on to Thirty-fifth Street, cut across to Madison Avenue, down to Thirty-third Street, then back to Fifth Avenue and past Thirty-fourth Street again, going uptown. The guy with the gripsack caught us first crack out of the box. "

"And then? " demanded the detective eagerly.

"I went on up Fifth Avenue, according to sailing orders, and the guy inside stopped me at Sixty-seventh Street. He got out and gimme a five-spot, telling me to go a few blocks, then turn and bring the lady back to the Sixth Avenue 'L' at Fifty-eighth Street. I done it. That's all. She went up the steps, and that's the last I seen of her. "

"Did she carry a small gripsack? "

"Yep. It would hold about as much as a high hat. "

Explicit as the information was it led nowhere, apparently. Mr. Birnes readily understood this much, yet there was a chance—a bare chance—that he might trace the girl on the 'L, ' in which case—anyway, it was worth trying.

"What did she look like? How was she dressed? " he asked.

"She had on one of them blue tailor-made things with a lid to match, and a long feather in it, " the cabby answered obligingly. "She was pretty as a—as a—she was a beaut, Cap, sort of skinny, and had all sorts of hair on her head—brownish, goldish sort of hair. She was about twenty-two or three, maybe, and—and—Cap, she was the goods, that's all. "

In the course of a day a thousand women, more or less, answering that description in a general sort of way, ride back and forth on the elevated trains. Mr. Birnes sighed as he remembered this; still it might produce results. Then came another idea.

"Did you happen to look in the cab after the young woman left it? " he inquired.

"No. "

"Had any fares since? "

"No. "

Mr. Birnes opened the door of the closed cab and glanced in. Perhaps there might be a stray glove, a handkerchief, some more definite clew than this vague description. He scrutinized the inside of the vehicle carefully; there was nothing. Yes, by Jingo, here was something—a white streak under the edge of the cushion on the seat! Mr. Birnes' hopeful fingers fished it out. It was a white envelope, sealed and—and addressed to him!

If you are as clever as I imagine you are, you will find this. My address is No. —— East Thirty-seventh Street. I shall be pleased to see you if you will call. E. VAN CORTLANDT WYNNE.

It was most disconcerting, really.

CHAPTER VII

A WINGED MESSENGER

A snow-white pigeon dropped down out of an azure sky and settled on a top-most girder of the great Singer Building. For a time it rested there, with folded pinions, in a din of clanging hammers; and a workman far out on a delicately balanced beam of steel paused in his labors to regard the bird with friendly eyes. The pigeon returned his gaze unafraid.

"Well, old chap, if I had as little trouble getting up here and down again as you do I wouldn't mind the job, " the workman remarked cheerfully.

The pigeon cooed an answer. The steel worker extended a caressing hand, whereupon the bird rose swiftly, surely, with white wings widely stretched, circled once over the vast steel structure, then darted away to the north. The workman watched the snow-white speck until it was lost against the blue sky, then returned to his labors.

Some ten minutes later Mr. E. van Cortlandt Wynne, sitting at a desk in his Thirty-seventh Street house, was aroused from his meditations by the gentle tinkle of a bell. He glanced up, arose, and went up the three flights of stairs to the roof. Half a dozen birds rose and fluttered around him as he opened the trap; one door in their cote at the rear of the building was closed. Mr. Wynne opened this door, reached in and detached a strip of tissue paper from the leg of a snow-white pigeon. He unfolded it eagerly; on it was written: Safe. I love you. D.

CHAPTER VIII

SOME CONJECTURES

Mr. Gustave Schultze dropped in to see Mr. Latham after luncheon, and listened with puckered brows to a recital of the substance of the detective's preliminary report, made the afternoon before.

"Mr. Birnes left here rather abruptly, " Mr. Latham explained in conclusion, "saying he would see me again, either last night or to-day. He has not appeared yet, and it may be that when he comes he will be able to add materially to what we now know. "

The huge German sat for a time with vacant eyes.

"Der gread question, Laadham, " he observed at last, gravely, "iss vere does Vynne ged dem. "

"I know that—I know it, " said Mr. Latham impatiently. "That is the very question we are trying to solve. "

"Und if we don'd solve him, Laadham, ve'll haf to do vatever as he says, " Mr. Schultze continued slowly. "Und ve may haf to do vatever as he says, anywhow. "

"Put one hundred million dollars into diamonds in one year—just the five of us? " demanded the other. "It's preposterous. "

"Id iss brebosterous, " the German agreed readily; "but das iss no argument. " He was silent for a little while. "Vere does he ged dem? Vere does he ged dem? " he repeated thoughtfully. "Do you believe, Laadham, it vould be bossible to smuggle in dwenty, d'irty, ein hundred million dollars of diamonds? "

"Certainly not, " was the reply.

"Den, if dey were nod smuggled in, dey are somewhere on der records of der Custom House, ain'd id? "

Mr. Latham snapped his fingers with a sudden realization of this possibility.

"Schultze, I believe that is our clew! " he exclaimed keenly. "Certainly they would have been listed by the customs department; and come to think of it, the tariff on them would have been enormous, so enormous that—that—" and he lost the hopeful tone—"so enormous that we must have heard of it when it became a matter of public record. "

"Yah, " Mr. Schultze agreed. "Diamonds like dose dupligates of der Koh-i-noor, der Orloff und der Regent could never haf passed through der Custom House, Laadham, mitoud attracting attention, so? "

Mr. Latham acquiesced by a nod of his head; Mr. Schultze sat regarding him through half-closed eyelids.

"Und if dey are nod on der Custom House records, " he continued slowly, "und dey are nod smuggled in, den, Laadham, den—Mein Gott, man, don'd you see? "

"See what? "

"Den dey are produced in dis country! "

For a minute or two Mr. Latham sat perfectly still, gazing into the other's eyes. First he was startled, then this gave way to incredulity, and at last he shook his head.

"No, " he said flatly. "No. "

"Laadham, ve Amerigans produce anyding, " the German went on patiently. "In eighdeen hundred und forty-eight ve didn't know California vas full of gold; und so late as eighdeen hundred und ninedy-four ve didn't know der Klondike vas full of gold. Der greadest diamond fields ve know now are in Africa, bud in eighdeen hundred und sixty-six ve didn't know id! Dere iss no reason ve should nod produce diamonds. "

"But look here, Schultze, " Mr. Latham expostulated, "it's—it's unheard of. "

"So vas der Mizzizzippi River until id was discovered, " the German argued complacently. "You are a diamond dealer, Laadham, bud you don'd know much aboud dem from whey dey come at. Iss

Czenki here? Send for him. He knows more aboud diamonds as any man vat ever lived. "

Mr. Latham sent an office boy for Czenki, who a few minutes later appeared with an inquiry in his beady black eyes and a nod of recognition for Mr. Schultze.

"Sid down, Mr. Czenki, " the German invited. "Sid down und draw a long breath, und den dell Mr. Laadham here someding aboud diamonds. "

"What is it, please? " Mr. Czenki asked of Mr. Latham.

"Mr. Czenki, have you any very definite idea as to where those diamonds came from? " asked Mr. Latham.

"No, " was the unhesitating response.

"Is it possible that they might have been found in the—in the United States? " Mr. Latham went on.

"Certainly. They might have been found anywhere. "

"As a matter of fact, were any diamonds ever found in the United States? "

"Yes, frequently. One very large diamond was found in 1855 at Manchester, across the James River from Richmond, Virginia. It weighed twenty-four carats when cut, and is the largest, I believe, ever found in this country. "

Mr. Latham seemed surprised.

"Why, you astonish me, " he remarked.

"Vait a minute und he'll astonish you some more, " Mr. Schultze put in confidently. "Vere else in der United States haf diamonds been found, Czenki? "

"In California, in North Carolina, and in Hall County, Georgia, " replied the expert readily. "There is good ground for the belief that the stone found at Richmond had been washed down from the mountains farther in the interior, and, if this is true, there is a substantial basis for the scientific hypothesis that diamond fields lie somewhere in the Appalachian Range, because the diamonds found in both North Carolina and Georgia were adjacent to these mountains. " He paused a moment. "This is all a matter of record. "

His employer was leaning forward in his chair, gripping the arms fiercely as he stared at him.

"Do you believe it possible, Mr. Czenki, " he asked deliberately, "that Mr. Wynne has found these diamond fields? "

The expert shrugged his slender shoulders.

"It is possible, of course, " he replied. "From time to time great sums of money have been spent in searching for them, so—" He waved his hand and was silent.

"Zo you see, Laadham, " Mr. Schultze interpolated, "ve don'd know anyding much. Ve know der African fields, und der Australian fields, und der Brazilian fields, und der fields in India, bud ve don'd know if new fields haf been found. By der time you haf lived so long as me you won't know any more as I do. "

There was silence for a long time. Mr. Czenki sat with impassive face, and his hands at rest on the arms of the chair. At last he spoke:

"If you'll pardon me, Mr. Latham, I may suggest another possibility. "

"Vas iss? " demanded Mr. Schultze quickly.

"Did you ever hear of the French scientist, Charles Friedel? " Mr. Czenki asked, addressing Mr. Latham.

"Never, no. "

"Well, this idea has occurred to me. Some years ago he discovered two or three small diamonds in a meteor. We may safely assume, from the fact that there were diamonds in one meteor, that there may be diamonds in other meteors, therefore—"

The German importer anticipated his line of thought and arose with a guttural burst of Teutonic expletives.

"Therefore, " the expert went on steadily, "is it not possible that Mr. Wynne has stumbled upon a huge deposit of diamonds in some meteoric substance some place in this country? A meteor may have fallen anywhere, of course, and it may have been only two months ago, or it may have been two thousand years ago. It may even be buried in his cellar. "

The huge German nodded his head vigorously, with sparkling eyes.

"It seems extremely probable that if diamond fields had been discovered in the Appalachian Range, " Mr. Czenki went on, "it would have become public in spite of every effort to prevent it; whereas, it is possible that a meteor containing diamonds might have been hidden away easily; and, also, the production of diamonds from such a source in this country would not make it necessary for the diamonds to pass through the Custom House. Is it clear, sir? "

"Why, it's absurd, fantastic, chimerical! " Mr. Latham burst out irritably. "It's ridiculous to consider such a thing. "

"I beg your pardon, " Mr. Czenki apologized. "It is only a conjecture, of course. I may add that I don't believe that three stones of the size of the replicas which Mr. Wynne produced here could have been found anywhere in the world and brought in here— smuggled in or in the usual way—and the secret held against the thousands of men who daily watch the diamond fields and market. It would not be difficult, however, if one man alone knew the source of the stones, to keep it from the world at large. I beg your pardon, " he added.

He arose as if to go. Mr. Schultze brought a heavy hand down on the slim shoulder of the expert, and turned to Mr. Latham.

"Laadham, you are listening to der man who knows more as all of us pud in a crowd, " he declared. "Mein Gott, I do believe he's right! "

Mr. Latham was a cold, unimaginative man of business; he hadn't even believed in fairies when he was a boy. This was child-talk; he permitted himself to express his opinion by a jerk of his head, and was silent. Diamonds like those out of meteors! Bosh!

CHAPTER IX

AND MORE DIAMONDS!

There was a rap on the door, and a clerk thrust his head in.

"Mr. Birnes to see you, sir, " he announced.

"Show him in, " directed Mr. Latham. "Sit down, both of you, and let's see what he has to say. "

There was an odd expression of hope deferred on the detective's face when he entered. He glanced inquiringly at Mr. Schultze and Mr. Czenki, whereupon Mr. Latham introduced them.

"You may talk freely, " he added. "We are all interested alike. "

The detective crossed his legs and balanced his hat carefully on a knee, the while he favored Mr. Czenki with a sharp scrutiny. There was that in the thin, scarred face and in the beady black eyes which inevitably drew the attention of a stranger, and half a dozen times as he talked Mr. Birnes glanced at the expert.

He retold the story of the cab ride up Fifth Avenue, and the car trip back downtown—omitting embarrassing details such as the finding of two notes addressed to himself—dwelt a moment upon the empty gripsack which Mr. Wynne carried on the car, and then:

"When you told me, Mr. Latham, that the gripsack had contained diamonds when Mr. Wynne left here I knew instantly how he got rid of them. He transferred them to some person in the cab, in accordance with a carefully prearranged plan. That person was a woman! "

"A woman! " Mr. Latham repeated, as if startled.

"Dere iss alvays wimmins in id, " remarked Mr. Schultze philosophically. "Go on. "

Mr. Birnes was not at all backward about detailing the persistence and skill it had required on his part to establish this fact; and he went on at length to acquaint them with the search that had been made by a dozen of his men to find a trace of the woman from the time she climbed the elevated stairs at Fifty-eighth Street. He admitted that the quest for her had thus far been fruitless, assuring them at the same time that it would go steadily on, for the present at least.

"And now, Mr. Latham, " he went on, and inadvertently he glanced at Mr. Czenki, "I have been hampered, of course, by the fact that you have not taken me completely into your confidence in this matter. I mean, " he added hastily, "that beyond a mere hint of their value I know nothing whatever about the diamonds which Mr. Wynne had in the gripsack. I gathered, however, that they were worth a large sum of money—perhaps, even a million dollars? "

"Yah, a million dollars ad leasd, " remarked Mr. Schultze grimly.

"Thank you, " and the detective smiled shrewdly. "Your instructions were to find where he got them. If there had been a theft of a million dollars' worth of diamonds anywhere in this world, I would have known it; so I took steps to examine the Custom House records of this and other cities to see if there had been an unusual shipment to Mr. Wynne, or to any one else outside of the diamond dealers, thinking this might give me a clew. "

"And what was the result? " demanded Mr. Latham quickly.

"My agents have covered all the Atlantic ports and they did not come in through the Custom House, " replied Mr. Birnes. "I have not heard from the western agents as yet, but my opinion is—is that they were perhaps smuggled in. Smuggling, after all, is simple with the thousands of miles of unguarded coasts of this country. I don't know this, of course; I advance it merely as a possibility. "

Mr. Latham turned to Mr. Schultze and Mr. Czenki with a triumphant smile. Diamonds in meteors! Tommyrot!

"Of course, " the detective resumed, "the whole investigation centers about this man Wynne. He has been under the eyes of my agents as no other man ever was, and in spite of this has been able to keep in correspondence with his accomplices. And, gentlemen, he has done it not through the mails, not over the telephone, not by telegraph, and yet he has done it. "

"By wireless, perhaps? " suggested Mr. Czenki. It was the first time he had spoken, and the detective took occasion then and there to stare at him frankly.

"And not by wireless, " he said at last. "He sends and receives messages from the roof of his house in Thirty-seventh Street by homing pigeons! "

"Some more fandastics, eh, Laadham? " Mr. Schultze taunted. "Some more chimericals? "

"I demonstrate this much by the close watch I have kept of Mr. Wynne, " the detective went on, there being no response to his questioning look at Mr. Schultze. "One of my agents, stationed on the roof of the house adjoining Mr. Wynne's" (it was the maid-servant next door) "has, on at least one occasion, seen him remove a tissue-paper strip from a carrier pigeon's leg and read what was written on it, after which he kissed it, gentlemen, kissed it; then he destroyed it. What did it mean? It means that that particular message was from the girl to whom he transferred the diamonds in the cab, and that he is madly in love with her. "

"Oh, dese wimmins! I dell you! " commented Mr. Schultze.

There was a little pause, then Mr. Birnes continued impressively:

"This correspondence is of no consequence in itself, of course. But it gives us this: Carrier pigeons will only fly home, so if Mr. Wynne received a message by pigeon it means that at some time, within a week say, he has shipped that pigeon and perhaps others from the house in Thirty-seventh Street to that person who sent him the message. If he sends messages to that person it means that he has received a pigeon or pigeons from that person within a week. And how were these pigeons shipped? In all probability, by express. So, gentlemen, you see there ought to be a record in the express offices, which would give us the home town, even the name and address, of the person who now has the diamonds in his or her keeping. Is that clear to all of you? "

"It is perfectly clear, " commented Mr. Laadham admiringly, while the German nodded his head in approval.

"And that is the clew we are working on at the moment, " the detective added. "Three of my men are now searching the records of all the express companies in the city—and there are a great many—for the pigeon shipments. If, as seems probable, this clew develops, it may be that we can place our hands on the diamonds within a few days. "

"I don'd d'ink I vould yust blace my hands on dem, " Mr. Schultze advised. "Dey are his diamonds, you know, und your hands might ged in drouble. "

"I mean figuratively, of course, " the detective amended.

He stopped and drummed on his stiff hat with his fingers. Again he glanced at the impassive face of Mr. Czenki with keen, questioning eyes; and for one bare instant it seemed as if he were trying to bring his memory to his aid.

"I've found out all about this man Wynne, " he supplemented after a moment, "but nothing in his record seems to have any bearing on this case. He is an orphan. His mother was a Van Cortlandt of old Dutch stock, and his father was a merchant downtown. He left a few thousands to the son, and the son is now in business for himself with an office in lower Broad Street. He is an importer of brown sugar. "

"Brown sugar? " queried Mr. Czenki quickly, and the thin, scarred face reflected for a second some subtle emotion within him. "Brown sugar! " he repeated.

"Yes, " drawled the detective, with an unpleasant stare, "brown sugar. He imports it from Cuba and Porto Rico and Brazil by the shipload, I understand, and makes a good thing of it. "

A quick pallor overspread Mr. Czenki's countenance, and he arose with his fingers working nervously. His beady eyes were glittering; his lips were pressed together until they were bloodless.

"Vas iss? " demanded Mr. Schultze curiously.

"My God, gentlemen, don't you see? " the expert burst out violently. "Don't you see what this man has done? He has—he has—"

Suddenly, by a supreme effort, he regained control of himself, and resumed his seat.

"He has—what? " asked Mr. Latham.

For half a minute Czenki stared at his employer; then his face grew impassive again.

"I beg your pardon, " he said quietly. "Mr. Wynne is a heavy importer of sugar from Brazil. Isn't it possible that those are Brazilian diamonds? That new workings have been discovered somewhere in the interior? That he has smuggled them in concealed in the sugar-bags, right into New York, under the noses of the customs officials? I beg your pardon, " he concluded.

Late in the afternoon of the following day a drunken man, unshaven, unkempt, unclean and clothed in rags, lurched into a small pawnshop in the lower Bowery and planked down on the dirty counter a handful of inert, colorless pebbles, ranging in size from a pea to a peanut.

"Say, Jew, is them real diamonds? " he demanded thickly.

The man in charge glanced at them and nearly fainted. Ten minutes later Red Haney, knight of the road, was placed under arrest as a suspicious character. Uncut diamonds, valued roughly at fifty thousand dollars, were found in his possession.

"Where did you get them? " demanded the amazed police.

"Found 'em. "

"Where did you find them? "

"None o' your business. "

And that was all they were able to get out of him at the moment.

CHAPTER X

THE BIG GAME

When the police of Mulberry Street find themselves face to face with some problem other than the trivial, every-day theft, burglary or murder, as the case may be, they are wont to rise up and run around in a circle. The case of Red Haney and the diamonds, blared to the world at large in the newspapers of Sunday morning, immediately precipitated a circular parade, while Haney, the objective center, snored along peacefully in a drunken stupor.

The statement of the case in the public press was altogether negative. There had been no report of the theft of fifty thousand dollars' worth of uncut diamonds in any city of the United States; in fact, diamonds, as a commodity in crime, had not figured in police records for several weeks—not even an actress had mislaid a priceless necklace. The newspapers were unanimously certain that stones of such value could not rightfully belong to a man of Haney's type, therefore, to whom did they belong?

Four men, at least, of the thousands who read the detailed account of the affair Sunday morning, immediately made it a matter of personal interest to themselves. One of these was Mr. Latham, another was Mr. Schultze, and a third was Mr. Birnes. The fourth was Mr. E. van Cortlandt Wynne. In the seclusion of his home in Thirty-seventh Street, Mr. Wynne read the story with puckered brows, then re-read it, after which he paced back and forth across his room in troubled thought for an hour or more. An oppressive sense of uneasiness was coming over him; and it was reflected in eyes grown somber.

After a time, with sudden determination, the young man dropped into a chair at his desk, and wrote in duplicate, on a narrow strip of tough tissue-paper, just one line:

Are you safe? Is all well? Answer quick. W.

Then he mounted to the roof. As he flung open the trap a man on the top of the house next door darted behind a chimney. Mr. Wynne saw him clearly—it was Frank Claflin—but he seemed to consider the matter of no consequence, for he paid not the slightest attention. Instead he went straight to a cage beside the pigeon-cote, wherein a dozen or more birds were imprisoned, removed one of them, attached a strip of the tissue-paper to its leg, and allowed it to rise from his out-stretched hand.

The pigeon darted away at an angle, up, up, until it grew indistinct against the void, then swung widely in a semicircle, hovered uncertainly for an instant, and flashed off to the west, straight as an arrow flies. Mr. Wynne watched it thoughtfully until it had disappeared; and Claflin's interest was so intense that he forgot the necessity of screening himself, the result being that when he turned again toward Mr. Wynne he found that young man gazing at him.

Mr. Wynne even nodded in a friendly sort of way as he attached the second strip of tissue to the leg of another bird. This rose, as the other had done, and sped away toward the west.

"It may be worth your while to know, Mr. Claflin, " Mr. Wynne remarked easily to the detective on the other house, "that if you ever put your foot on this roof to intercept any message which may come to me I shall shoot you. "

Then he turned and went down the stairs again, closing and locking the trap in the roof behind him. He should get an answer to those questions in two hours, three hours at the most. If there was no answer within that time he would despatch more birds, and then, if no answer came, then—then—Mr. Wynne sat down and carefully perused the newspaper story again.

At just about that moment the attention of one John Sutton, another of the watchful Mr. Birnes' men, on duty in Thirty-seventh Street, was attracted to a woman who had turned in from Park Avenue, and was coming rapidly toward him, on the opposite side of the street. She was young, with the elasticity of perfect health in her step; and closely veiled. She wore a blue tailor-made gown, with hat to match; and recalcitrant strands of hair gleamed a golden brown.

"By George! " exclaimed the detective. "It's her! "

By which he meant that the mysterious young woman of the cab, whose description had been drilled into him by Mr. Birnes, had at last reappeared. He lounged along the street, watching her with keen interest, fixing her every detail in his mind. She did not hesitate, she glanced neither to right nor left, but went straight to the house occupied by Mr. Wynne, and rang the bell. A moment later the door was opened, and she disappeared inside. The detective mopped his face with tremulous joy.

"Doris! " exclaimed Mr. Wynne, as the veiled girl entered the room where he sat. "Doris, my dear girl, what are you doing here? "

He arose and went toward her. She tore off the heavy veil impatiently, and lifted her moist eyes to his. There was suffering in them, uneasiness—and more than that.

"Have you heard from him—out there? " she demanded.

"Not to-day, no, " he responded. "Why did you come here? "

"Gene, I can't stand it, " she burst out passionately. "I'm worried to death. I can't hear a word, and—I'm worried to death. "

Mr. Wynne wondered if she, too, had seen the morning papers. He stared at her gravely for an instant, then turned, crumpled up the section of newspaper with its glaring head-lines and dropped it into a waste-basket.

"I'm sorry, " he said gently.

"I telephoned twice yesterday, " she rushed on quickly, pleadingly, "and once last night and again this morning. There was no—no answer. Gene, I couldn't stand it. I had to come. "

"It's only that he didn't happen to be within hearing of the telephone bell, " he assured her. But her steadfast, accusing eyes read more than that in his face, and her hands trembled on his arm.

"I'm afraid, Gene, I'm afraid, " she declared desperately. "Suppose— suppose something has happened? "

"It's absurd, " and he attempted to laugh off her uneasiness. "Why, nothing could have happened. "

"All those millions of dollars' worth of diamonds, Gene, " she reminded him, "and he is—I shouldn't have left him alone. "

"Why, my dear Doris, " and Mr. Wynne gathered the slender, trembling figure in his arms protectingly, "not one living soul, except you and I, knows that they are there. There's no incentive to robbery, my dear—a poor, shabby little cottage like that. There is not the slightest danger. "

"There is always danger, Gene, " she contradicted. "It makes me shudder just to think of it. He is so old and so feeble, simple as a child, and utterly helpless if anything should happen. Then, when I didn't hear from him after trying so many times over the telephone —I'm afraid, Gene, I'm afraid, " she concluded desperately.

The long-pent-up tears came, and she buried her face on his shoulder. He stood silent, with narrowed, thoughtful eyes.

This, and the thing in the newspaper there! And evidently she had not seen that! It was not wise that she should see it just yet.

"That day I took the horrid things from you in the cab I was awfully frightened, " she continued sobbingly. "I felt that every one I passed knew I had them; and you can't imagine what a relief it was when I took them back out there and left them. And now when I think that something may have happened to him! " She paused, then raised her tear-dimmed eyes to his face. "He is all I have in the world now, Gene, except you. Already the hateful things have cost the lives of my father and my brother, and now if he—Or you—Oh, my God, it would kill me! I hate them, hate them! "

She was shaken by a paroxysm of sobs. Mr. Wynne led her to a chair, and she dropped into it wearily, with her face in her hands.

"Nothing can have happened, Doris, " he repeated gently. "I sent a message out there in duplicate only a few minutes ago. In a couple of hours, now, we shall be getting an answer. Now, don't begin to cry, " he added helplessly.

"And if you don't get an answer? " she insisted.

"I shall get an answer, " he declared positively. There was a long pause. "And when I get that answer, Doris, " he resumed, again becoming very grave, "you will see how unwise, how dangerous even, it was for you to come here this way. I know it's hard, dear, " he supplemented apologetically, "but it was only for the week, you know; and now I don't see how you can go away from here again. "

"Go away? " she repeated wonderingly. "Why shouldn't I go away? I was very careful to veil myself when I came—no one saw me enter, I am sure. Why can't I go away again? "

Mr. Wynne paced the length of the room twice, with troubled brow.

"You don't understand, dear, " he said quietly, as he paused before her. "From the moment I left Mr. Latham's office last Thursday I have been under constant surveillance. I'm followed wherever I go— to my office, to luncheon, to the theater, everywhere; and day and night, day and night, there are two men watching this house, and two other men watching at my office. They tamper with my correspondence, trace my telephone calls, question my servants, quiz my clerks. You don't understand, dear, " he said again.

"But why should they do all this? " she asked curiously. "Why should they—"

"I had expected it all, of course, " he interrupted, "and it doesn't disturb me in the least. I planned for months to anticipate every emergency; I know every detective who is watching me by name and by sight; and all my plans have gone perfectly until now. This is why it was necessary for me to keep away from out there as it was for you to keep away from here; why we could not afford to take chances by an interchange of letters or by telephone calls. When I left you in the cab I knew you would get away safely, because they did not know you were there, in the first place; and then it was the beginning of the chase and I forced them to center their attention on me. But now it different. Come here to the window a minute. "

He led her across the room unresistingly. On the opposite side of the street, staring at the house, was a man.

"That man is a private detective, " Mr. Wynne informed her. "His name is Sutton, and he is only one of thirty or forty whose sole business in life, right now, is to watch me, to keep track of and follow any person who comes here. He saw you enter, and you couldn't escape him going out. There's another on the roof of the house next door. His name is Claflin. These men, or others from the same agency, are here all the time. There are two more at my office downtown; still others are searching customs records, examining the books of the express companies, probing into my private affairs. And they're all in the employ of the men with whom I am dealing. Do you understand now? "

"I didn't dream of such a thing, " the girl faltered slowly. "I knew, of course, that—Gene, I shouldn't have come if—if only I could have heard from him. "

"My dear girl, it's a big game we are playing—a hundred-million-dollar game! And we shall win it, unless—we shall win it, in spite of them. Naturally the diamond dealers don't want to be compelled to put up one hundred million dollars. They reason that if the stones I showed them came from new fields, and the supply is unlimited, as I told them, that the diamond market is on the verge of collapse, anyway; and as they look at it they are compelled to know where they came from. As a matter of fact, if they did know, or if the public got one inkling of the truth, the diamond market would be wrecked, and all the diamond dealers in the world working together couldn't prevent it. If they succeed in doing this thing they feel they must do, they will only bring disaster upon themselves. It would do no good to tell them so; I merely laid my plans and am letting them alone. So, you see, my dear, it is a big game—a big game! "

CHAPTER XI

THE SILENT BELL

He stood looking at her with earnest thoughtful eyes. Suddenly the woman-soul within her awoke in a surging, inexplicable wave of emotion which almost overcame her; and after it came something of realization of the great fight he was making for her—for her, and the aged, feeble grandfather waiting patiently out there. He loved her, this master among men, and she sighed contentedly. For the moment the maddening anxiety that brought her here was forgotten; there was only the ineffable sweetness of seeing him again. She extended her hands to him impulsively, and he kissed them both.

"The difficulty of you leaving here, " he went on after a little, "is that you would be followed, and within two hours these men would know all about you—where you are stopping, how long you have been there; they would know of your daily telephone messages to your grandfather, and then, inevitably, they would appear out there, and learn all the rest of it. It doesn't matter how closely they keep watch of me. My plans are all made, I know I am watched, and make no mistakes. But you! "

"So I should not have come? " she questioned. "I'm sorry. "

"I understand your anxiety, of course, " he assured her, and he was smiling a little, "but the worst never happens—so for the present we will not worry. In an hour or more, now, I imagine we shall receive a pigeon-o-gram which will show that all is well. And then I shall have to plan for you to get away somehow. "

She leaned toward him a little and again he gathered her in his arms. The red lips were mutely raised, and he kissed her reverently.

"It's all for you and it will all be right, " he assured her.

"Gene, dear Gene! "

He pressed a button on the wall and a maid appeared.

"You will have to wait for a couple of hours or so, at least, so if you would like to take off your things? " he suggested with grave courtesy. "I dare say the suite just above is habitable, and the maid is at your service. "

The girl regarded him pensively for a moment, then turning ran swiftly up the stairs. The maid started to follow more staidly.

"Just a moment, " said Mr. Wynne crisply, in an undertone. "Miss Kellner is not to be allowed to use the telephone under any circumstances. You understand? " She nodded silently and went up the stairs.

An hour passed. From the swivel chair at his desk Mr. Wynne had twice seen Sutton stroll past on the opposite side of the street; and then Claflin had lounged along. Suddenly he arose and went to the window, throwing back the curtains. Sutton was leaning against an electric-light pole, half a block away; Claflin was half a block off in the other direction, in casual conversation with a policeman. Mr. Wynne looked them over thoughtfully. Curiously enough he was wondering just how he would fare in a physical contest with either, or both.

He turned away from the window at last and glanced at his watch impatiently. One hour and forty minutes! In another half an hour the little bell over his desk should ring. That would mean that a pigeon had arrived from—from out there, and that the automatic door had closed upon it as it entered the cote. But if it didn't come— if it didn't come! Then what? There was only one conclusion to be drawn, and he shuddered a little when he thought of it. There could only remain this single possibility when he considered the sinister things that had happened—the failure of the girl to get an answer by telephone, and the unexpected appearance of Red Haney with the uncut diamonds. It might be necessary for him to go out there, and how could he do it? How, without leaving an open trail behind him? How, without inviting defeat in the fight he was making?

His meditations were interrupted by the appearance of Miss Kellner. She had crept down the stairs noiselessly, and stood beside him before he was aware of her presence. Her eyes sought his countenance questioningly, and the deadly pallor of her face frightened him. She crept into his arms and nestled there silently with dry, staring eyes. He stroked the golden-brown hair with an utter sense of helplessness.

"Nothing yet, " he said finally, and there was a thin assumption of cheeriness in his tone. "It may be another hour, but it will come— it will come. "

"But if it doesn't, Gene? " she queried insistently. Always her mind went back to that possibility.

"We shall cross no bridges until we reach them, " he replied. "There is always a chance that the pigeons might have gone astray, for they have this single disadvantage against the incalculable advantage of offering no clew to any one as to where they go; and it is impossible to follow them. If nothing comes in half an hour now I shall send two more. "

"And then, if nothing comes? "

"Then, my dear, then we shall begin to worry. "

Half an hour passed; the little bell was silent; Claflin and Sutton were still visible from the window. Miss Kellner's eyes were immovably fixed on Mr. Wynne's face, and he repressed his gnawing anxiety with an effort. Finally he wrote again on the tissue slips— three of them this time—and together they climbed to the roof, attached the messages, and watched the birds disappear.

Another hour—two hours—two hours and a half passed. Suddenly the girl arose with pallid face and colorless lips.

"I can't stand it, Gene, I can't! " she exclaimed hysterically. "I must know. The telephone? "

"No, " he commanded harshly, and he, too, arose. "No. "

"I will! " she flashed.

She darted out of the room and along the hall. He followed her with grim determination in his face. She seized the receiver from the hook and held it to her ear.

"Hello! " called Central.

"Give me long distance—Coaldale, Number—"

"No, " commanded Mr. Wynne, and he placed one hand over the transmitter tightly. "Doris, you must not! "

"I will! " she flamed. "Let me alone! "

"You'll ruin everything, " he pleaded earnestly. "Don't you know that they get every number I call? Don't you know that within fifteen minutes they will have that number, and their men will start for there? "

She faced him with blazing eyes.

"I don't care, " she said deliberately, and the white face was relieved by an angry flush. "I will know what has happened out there! I must! Gene, don't you see that I'm frantic with anxiety? The money means nothing to me. I want to know if he is safe. "

His hand was still gripped over the transmitter. Suddenly she turned and tugged at it fiercely. Her sharp little nails bit into the flesh of his fingers. In a last desperate effort she placed the receiver to her lips.

"Give me long distance, Coaldale Number—"

With a quick movement he snapped the connecting wire from the instrument, and the receiver was free in her hand.

"Doris, you are mad! " he protested. "Wait a minute, my dear girl— just a minute. "

"I don't care! I will know! "

Mr. Wynne turned and picked up a heavy cane from the hall-stand, and brought it down on the transmitter with all his strength. The delicate mechanism jangled and tingled, then the front fell off at their feet. The diaphragm dropped and rolled away.

"Doris, you must not! " he commanded again gravely. "We will find another way, dear. "

"How dare you? " she demanded violently. "It was cowardly. "

"You don't understand—"

"I understand it all, " she broke in. "I understand that this might lead to the failure of the thing you are trying to do. But I don't care. I understand that already I have lost my father and my brother in this; that my grandmother and my mother were nearly starved to death while it was all being planned; all for these hideous diamonds. Diamonds! Diamonds! Diamonds! I've heard nothing all my life but that. As a child it was dinned into me, and now I am sick and weary of it all. I know—I know something has happened to him now. I hate them! I hate them! "

She stopped, glared at him with scornful eyes for an instant, then ran up the stairs again. Mr. Wynne touched a button in the wall, and the maid appeared.

"Go lock the back door, and bring me the key, " he commanded.

The maid went away, and a moment later returned to hand him the key. He still stood in the hall, waiting.

After a little there came a rush of skirts, and Miss Kellner ran down the steps, dressed for the street.

"Doris, " he pleaded, "you must not go out now. Wait just a moment— we'll find a way, and then I'll go with you. "

She tried to pass him, but his outstretched arms made her a prisoner.

"Do I understand that you refuse to let me go? " she asked tensely.

"Not like this, " he replied. "If you'll give me just a little while then perhaps—perhaps I may go with you. Even if something had happened there you could do nothing alone. I, too, am afraid now. Just half an hour—fifteen minutes! Perhaps I may be able to find a plan. "

Suddenly she sank down on the stairs, with her face in her hands. He caressed her hair tenderly, then raised her to her feet.

"Suppose you step into the back parlor here, " he requested. "Just give me fifteen minutes. Then, unless I can find a way for us to go together safely, we will throw everything aside and go anyway. Forgive me, dear. "

She submitted quietly to be led along the hall. He opened the door into a room and stood aside for her to pass.

"Gene, Gene! " she exclaimed.

Her soft arms found their way about his neck, and she drew his face down and kissed him; then, without a word, she entered the room and closed the door. A minute passed—two, four, five—and Mr. Wynne stood as she left him, then he opened the front door and stepped out.

Frank Claflin was just starting toward the house from the corner with deliberate pace when he glanced up and saw Mr. Wynne signaling for him to approach. Could it be possible? He had had no orders about talking to this man, but—Perhaps he was going to give it up! And with this idea he accelerated his pace and crossed the street.

"Oh, Mr. Claflin, will you step in just a moment, please? " requested Mr. Wynne courteously.

"Why? " demanded the detective suspiciously.

"There's a matter I want to discuss with you, " responded Mr. Wynne. "It may be that we can reach some sort of—of an agreement about this, and if you don't mind—"

Claflin went up the steps, Mr. Wynne ushered him in and closed the door behind him.

Three minutes later Mr. Wynne appeared on the steps again and beckoned to Sutton, who had just witnessed the incident just preceding, and was positively being eaten by curiosity.

"This is Mr. Sutton, isn't it? " inquired Mr. Wynne.

"Yes, that's me. "

"Well, Mr. Claflin and I are discussing this matter, and my proposition to him was such that he felt if must be made in your presence. Would you mind stepping inside for a moment? "

"You and the girl decided to give it up? " queried Mr. Sutton triumphantly.

"We are just discussing the matter now, " was the answer.

Sutton went up the steps and disappeared inside.

And about four minutes after that Mr. Wynne stood in the hallway, puffing a little as he readjusted his necktie. He picked up his hat, drew on his gloves and then rapped on the door of the back parlor. Miss Kellner appeared.

"We will go now, " said Mr. Wynne quietly.

"But is it safe, Gene? " she asked quickly.

"Perfectly safe, yes. There's no danger of being followed if we go immediately. "

She gazed at him wonderingly, then followed him to the door. He opened it and she passed out, glancing around curiously. For one instant he paused, and there came a clatter and clamor from somewhere in the rear of the house. He closed the door with a grim smile.

"Which are the detectives? " asked Miss Kellner, in an awed whisper.

"I don't see them around just now, " he replied. "We can get a cab at the corner. "

CHAPTER XII

THE THIRD DEGREE

Some years ago a famous head of the police department clearly demonstrated the superiority of a knock-out blow, frequently administered, as against moral suasion, and from that moment the "third degree" became an institution. Whatever sort of criticism may be made of the "third degree, " it is, nevertheless, amazingly effective, and beyond that, affords infinite satisfaction to the administrator. There is a certain vicious delight in brutally smashing a sullen, helpless prisoner in the face; and the "third degree" is not officially in existence.

Red Haney was submitted to the "third degree. " His argument that he found the diamonds, and that having found them they were his until the proper owner appeared, was futile. Ten minutes after having passed into a room where sat Chief Arkwright, of the Mulberry Street force, and three of his men, and Steven Birnes, of the Birnes Detective Agency, Haney remembered that he hadn't found the diamonds at all—somebody had given them to him.

"Who gave them to you? " demanded the chief.

"I don't know the guy's name, Boss, " Haney replied humbly.

"This is to remind you of it. "

Haney found himself sprawling on the floor, and looked up, with a pleading, piteous expression. His eyes were still red and bleary, his motley face shot with purple, and the fumes of the liquor still clouded his brain. The chief stood above him with clenched fist.

"On the level, Boss, I don't know, " he whined.

"Get up! " commanded the chief. Haney struggled to his feet and dropped into his chair. "What does he look like—this man who gave them to you? Where did you meet him? Why did he give them to you? "

"Now, Boss, I'm goin' to give you the straight goods, " Haney pleaded. "Don't hit me any more an' I'll tell you all I know about it. "

The chief sat down again with scowling face. Haney drew a long breath of relief.

"He's a little, skinny feller, Boss, " the prisoner went on to explain, the while he thoughtfully caressed his jaw. "I meets him out here in a little town called Willow Creek, me havin' swung off a freight there to git somethin' to eat. He's just got a couple of handouts an' he passes one to me, an' we gits to talkin'. He gits to tellin' me somethin' about a nutty old gazebo who lives in the next town, which he had just left. This old bazoo, he says, has a hatful o' diamonds up there, but they ain't polished or nothin' an' he's there by hisself, an' is old an' simple, an' it's findin' money, he says, to go over an' take 'em away from him. He reckoned there must 'a' been a thousan' dollars' worth altogether.

"Well, he puts the proposition to me, " Haney continued circumstantially, "an' I falls for it. We're to go over, an' I'm to pipe it all off to see it's all right, then I'm to sort o' hang aroun' an' keep watch while he goes in an' gives the old nut a gentle tap on the coco, an' cops the sparks. That's what we done. I goes up an' takes a few looks aroun', then I whistles an' he appears from the back, an' goes up to the kitchen for a handout. The old guy opens the door, an' he goes in. About a minute later he comes out an' gives me a handful o' little rocks—them I had—an' we go away. He catches a freight goin' west, an' I swings one for Jersey City. "

"When was this? " demanded Chief Arkwright.

"What's to-day? " asked Haney in turn.

"This is Sunday morning. "

"Well, it was yesterday mornin' sometime, Saturday. When I gits to Jersey I takes one o' the little rocks an' goes into a place an' shows it to the bar-keep. He gives me a lot o' booze for it, an' I guess I gits considerable lit up, an' he also gives me some money to pay ferry fare, an' the next thing I knows I'm nabbed over in the hock-shop. I guess I was lit up good, 'cause if I'd 'a' been right I wouldn't 'a' went to the hock-shop an' got pinched. "

He glanced around at the five other men in the room, and he read belief in each face, whereupon he drew a breath of relief.

"What town was it? " asked the chief.

"Little place named Coaldale. "

"Coaldale, " the chief repeated thoughtfully. "Where is that? "

"About forty or fifty miles out'n Jersey" said Haney.

"I know the place, " remarked Mr. Birnes.

"You are sure, Haney? " said the chief after a pause. "You are sure you don't know this other man's name? "

"I don't know it, Boss. "

"Who was the man you robbed? "

"I don't know. "

The chief arose quickly, and the prisoner cringed in his seat.

"I don't know, " he went on protestingly. "Don't hit me again. "

But the chief had no such intention; it was merely to walk back and forth across the room.

"What kind of man was he—a tramp? "

Haney faltered and thoughtfully pulled his under-lip. The cunning brain behind the bleary eyes was working now.

"I wouldn't call him a tramp, " he said evasively. "He had on collar an' cuffs an' good clothes, an' talked sort o' easy. "

"Little, skinny man you said. What color was his hair? "

The chief turned in his tracks and regarded Haney with keen, inquiring eyes. The prisoner withstood the scrutiny bravely.

"Sort o' blackish, brownish hair. "

"Black, you mean? "

"Well, yes—black. "

"And his eyes? "

"Black eyes—little an' round like gimlet holes. "

"Heavy eyebrows, I suppose? "

"Yes, " Haney agreed readily. "They sort o' stuck out. "

"And his nose? Big or little? Heavy or thin? "

Haney considered that thoughtfully for a moment before he answered. Then:

"Sort o' medium nose, Boss, with a point on it. "

"And a thin face, naturally. How much did he weigh? "

"Oh, he was a little feller—skinny, you know. I reckon he didn't weigh no more'n a hundred an' twenty-five or thirty. "

Some germ had been born in the fertile mind of Mr. Birnes; now it burst into maturity. He leaned forward in his chair and stared coldly at Haney.

"Perhaps, " he suggested slowly, "perhaps he had a scar on his face? "

Haney returned the gaze dully for an instant, then suddenly he nodded his head.

"Yes, a scar, " he said.

"From here? " Mr. Birnes placed one finger on the point of his chin and drew it across his right jaw.

"Yes, a scar—that's it; " the prisoner acquiesced, "from his chin almost around to his ear. "

Mr. Birnes came to his feet, while the official police stared. The chief sat down again and crossed his fat legs.

"Why, what do you know, Birnes? " he queried.

"I know the man, Chief, " the detective burst out confidently. "I'd gamble my head on it. I knew it! I knew it! " he told himself. Again he faced the tramp: "Haney, do you know how much the diamonds you had were worth? "

"Must 'a' been three or four hundred dollars. "

"Something like fifty thousand dollars, " Mr. Birnes informed him impressively; "and if you got fifty thousand dollars for your share the other man got a million. "

Haney only stared.

CHAPTER XIII

MR. CZENKI APPEARS

Half an hour later Mr. Birnes, Chief Arkwright and Detective Sergeant Connelly were on a train, bound for Coaldale. Mr. Birnes had left them for a moment at the ferry and rushed into a telephone booth. When he came out he was exuberantly triumphant.

"It's my man, all right, " he assured the chief. "He has been missing since Friday night, and no one knows his whereabouts. It's my man. "

It was an hour's ride to Coaldale, a sprawling, straggly village with only four or five houses in sight from the station. When the three men left the train there, Mr. Birnes walked over and spoke to the agent, a thin, cadaverous, tobacco-chewing specimen of his species.

"We are looking for an old gentleman who lives out here somewhere, " he explained. "He probably lives alone, and we've been told that he has a little cottage somewhere over this way. "

He waved his hand vaguely to the right, in accordance with the directions of Red Haney. The station agent scratched his stubbly chin, and spat with great accuracy through a knot-hole ten feet away.

"'Spect you mean old man Kellner, " he replied obligingly. "He lives by hisself part of the time; then again sometimes his grand-darter lives with him. "

Granddaughter! Mr. Birnes almost jumped.

"A granddaughter, yes, " he said with a forced calm. "Rather a pretty girl, twenty-two or three years old? Sometimes she dresses in blue? "

"Yes, " the agent agreed. "'Spect them's them. Follow the road there till you come to Widow Gardiner's hog-lot, then turn to your left, and it's about a quarter of a mile on. The only house up that way— you can't miss it. "

The agent stood squinting at them, with friendly inquiry radiating from his parchment-like countenance, and Mr. Birnes took an opportunity to ask some other questions.

"By the way, what sort of old man is this Mr. Kellner? What does he do? Is he wealthy? "

A pleasant grin overspread his informant's face; one finger was raised to his head and twirled significantly.

"'Spect he's crazy, " he went on to explain. "Don't do nothing, so far as nobody knows—lives like a hermit, stays in the house all the time, and has long whiskers. Don't know whether he's rich or not, but 'spect he ain't becuz no man with money'd live like he does. " He thrust a long forefinger into Mr. Birnes' face. "And stingy! He's so stingy he won't let nobody come in the house—scared they'll wear the furniture out looking at it. "

"How long has he lived here? "

"There ain't nobody in this town old enough to say. Why, mister, I'll bet that old man's a thousand years old. Wait'll you see him. "

That was all. They went on as indicated.

"The very type of man who would scrimp and starve to put all his money in something like diamonds, " mused Chief Arkwright. "The usual rich old miser who winds up by being murdered. "

They passed the "Widow Gardiner's hog-lot" and came into a pleasant country road, which, turning, brought them to a shabby little cottage, embowered in trees. Through the foliage, farther on, they caught the amber gleam of a languid river; and around their feet, as they entered the yard, scores of pigeons fluttered.

"Carriers! " ejaculated Mr. Birnes, as if startled.

With a strange feeling of elation the detective led the way up the steps to the veranda and knocked. There was no answer. He glanced at the chief significantly, and tried the door. It was locked.

"Try the back door, " directed Chief Arkwright tersely. "If that's locked we'll go in anyway. "

They passed around the house to the rear, and Mr. Birnes laid one hand upon the door-knob. He turned it and the door swung inward. Again he glanced at Chief Arkwright. The chief nodded, and led the way into the house. They stood in a kitchen, clean as to floors and tables, but now in the utmost disorder. They spent only a moment here, then passed into the narrow hall, along this to a door that stood open, and then—then Chief Arkwright paused, staring downward, and respectfully lifted his hat.

"Always the same, " he remarked enigmatically.

Mr. Birnes thrust himself forward and through the door. On the floor, with white face turned upward, and fixed, staring eyes, lay an old man. His venerable gray hair, long and unkempt, fell back from a brow of noble proportions, the wide, high brow of the student; and a great, snow-white beard rippled down over his breast. Save for the glassiness of the eyes the face was placid in death, even as it must have been in life.

Mutely Mr. Birnes examined the body. A blow in the back of the head—that was all. Then he glanced around the room inquiringly. Everything was in order, except—except here lay an overturned cigar-box. He picked it up; two uncut diamonds were on the floor beneath it. The rough, inert pebbles silently attested the obvious manner of death which simultaneously forced itself upon the three men—the cowardly blow of an assassin, a dying struggle, perhaps, for the contents of the box, and this—the end!

From outside came sharply in the silence the rattle of wheels on the gravel of the road, and a vehicle stopped in front of the door.

"Sh-h-h-h! " warned the chief.

Some one came along the walk, up the steps and rapped briskly on the door; the detectives waited motionless, silent The knob rattled under impatient fingers, then the footsteps passed along the veranda quickly, and were lost, as if some one had stepped off at the end intending to come to the back door, which was open. A moment later they heard steps in the kitchen, then in the narrow hall approaching, and the doorway of the room where they stood framed the figure of a man. It was Mr. Czenki.

"There's your man, Chief, " remarked Mr. Birnes quietly.

The diamond expert permitted his gaze to wander from one to another of the three men, and then the beady black eyes came to rest on the silent, outstretched figure of the old man. He started forward impulsively; the grip of Detective-Sergeant Connelly on his arm stopped him.

"You're my prisoner! "

"Yes, I understand, " said Mr. Czenki impatiently. He didn't even look up; he was still gazing at the figure on the floor.

"Well, what have you got to say for yourself? " demanded Chief Arkwright coldly.

Mr. Czenki met the accusing stare of the chief squarely for an instant, then the keen eyes shifted to the slightly flushed face of Mr. Birnes and lingered there interrogatively.

"I have nothing whatever to say, " he replied at last, and he drew one hand slowly across his thin, scarred face. "Yes, I understand, " he repeated absently. "I have nothing to say. "

CHAPTER XIV

CAUGHT IN THE NET

Doris looked down in great, dry-eyed horror upon the body of this withered old man whom she had loved, and the thin thread of life within her all but snapped. It had come; the premonition of disaster had been fulfilled; the last of her blood had been sacrificed to the mercilessly glittering diamonds—father, brother and now him! Mr. Wynne's face went white, and his teeth closed fiercely; he had loved this old man, too; then the shock passed and he turned anxiously to Doris to receive the limp, inert figure in his arms. She had fainted.

"Well, what do you know about it? " inquired Chief Arkwright abruptly.

Mr. Wynne was himself again instantly—the calm, self-certain perfectly poised young man of affairs. He glanced at the chief, then shot a quick, inquiring look at Mr. Czenki. Almost imperceptibly the diamond expert shook his head. Then Mr. Wynne's eyes turned upon Mr. Birnes. There had been triumph in the detective's face until that moment, but, under the steady, meaning glare which was directed at him, triumph faded to a sort of wonder, followed by a vague sense of uneasiness, and he read a command in the fixed eyes—a command to silence. Curiously enough it reminded him that he was in the employ of Mr. Latham, and that there were certain business secrets to be protected. He regarded the coroner's physician, hastily summoned for a perfunctory examination.

"Well? " demanded the chief again.

"Nothing—of this, " replied Mr. Wynne. "I think, Doctor, " and he addressed the physician, "that she needs you more than he does. We know only too well what's the matter with him. "

The physician arose obediently. Mr. Wynne gathered up the slender, still figure in his arms, and bore it away to another room. The doctor bent over Doris, and tested the fluttering heart.

"Only shock, " he said finally, when he looked up. "She'll come round all right in a little while. "

"Thank God! " the young man breathed softly.

He stooped and pressed reverent lips to the marble-white brow, then straightened up and, after one long, lingering look at her, turned quickly and left the room.

"I have no statement to make, " Mr. Czenki was saying, in that level, unemotional way of his, when Mr. Wynne reentered the room where lay the dead.

"We are to assume that you are guilty, then? " demanded Chief Arkwright with cold finality.

"I have nothing to say, " replied the expert. His gaze met that of Mr. Wynne for a moment, then settled on the venerable face of the old man.

"Guilty? " interposed Mr. Wynne quickly. "Guilty of what? "

Chief Arkwright, without speaking, waved his hand toward the body on the floor. There was a flash of amazement in the young man's face, a sudden bewilderment; the diamond expert's countenance was expressionless.

"You don't deny that you killed him? " persisted the chief accusingly.

"I have nothing to say, " said the expert again.

"And you don't deny that you were Red Haney's accomplice? "

"I have nothing to say, " was the monotonous answer.

The chief shrugged his shoulders impatiently. Some illuminating thought shone for an instant in Mr. Wynne's clear eyes and he nodded as if a question in his mind had been answered.

"Perhaps, Chief, there may be some mistake? " he protested half-heartedly. "Perhaps this gentleman—what motive would—"

"There's motive enough, " interrupted the chief briskly. "We have this man's description straight from his accomplice, Red Haney, even to the scar on his face—" He paused abruptly, and regarded Mr.

Wynne through half-closed lids. "By the way, " he continued deliberately, "who are you? What do you know about it? "

"My name is Wynne—E. van Cortlandt Wynne" was the ready response. "I am directly interested in this case through a long-standing friendship for Mr. Kellner here, and through the additional fact that his granddaughter in the adjoining room is soon to become my wife. " There was a little pause. "I may add that I live in New York, and that Miss Kellner has been stopping there for several days. She has been accustomed to hearing from her grandfather at least once a day by telephone, but she was unable to get an answer either yesterday or to-day, so she came to my home, and together we came out here. "

Mr. Birnes looked up quickly. It had suddenly occurred to him to wonder as to the whereabouts of Claflin and Sutton, who had been on watch at the Thirty-seventh Street house. The young man interpreted the expression of his face aright, and favored him with a meaning glance.

"We came alone, " he supplemented.

Mr. Birnes silently pondered it.

"All that being true, " Chief Arkwright suggested tentatively, "perhaps you can give us some information as to the diamonds that were stolen? How much were they worth? How many were there? " He held up the uncut stones that had been found on the floor.

"I don't know their exact number, " was the reply. "Their value, I should say, was about sixty thousand dollars. Except for this little house, and the grounds adjoining, practically all of Mr. Kellner's money was invested in diamonds. Those you have there are part of an accumulation of many years, imported in the rough, one or two at a time. "

Mr. Czenki was gazing abstractedly out of a window, but the expression on his lean face indicated the keenest interest, and—and something else; apprehension, maybe. The chief stared straight into the young man's eyes for an instant, and then:

"And Mr. Kellner's family? " he inquired.

"There is no one, except his granddaughter, Doris. "

Some change, sudden as it was pronounced, came over the chief, and his whole attitude altered. He dropped into a chair near the door.

"Have a seat, Mr. Wynne, " he invited courteously, "and let's understand this thing clearly. Over there, please, " and he indicated a chair partly facing that in which Mr. Czenki sat.

Mr. Wynne sat down.

"Now you don't seem to believe, " the chief went on pleasantly, "that Czenki here killed Mr. Kellner? "

"Well, no, " the young man admitted.

Mr. Czenki glanced at him quickly, warningly. The chief was not looking, but he knew the glance had passed.

"And why don't you believe it? " he continued.

"In the first place, " Mr. Wynne began without hesitation, "the diamonds were worth only about sixty thousand dollars, and Mr. Czenki here draws a salary of twenty-five thousand dollars a year. The proportion is wrong, you see. Again, Mr. Czenki is a man of unquestioned integrity. As diamond expert of the Henry Latham Company he handles millions of dollars' worth of precious stones each year, and has practically unlimited opportunities for theft, without murder, if he were seeking to steal. He has been with that company for several years, and that fact alone is certainly to his credit. "

"Very good, " commented the chief ambiguously. He paused an instant to study this little man with an interest aroused by the sum of his salary. "And what of Haney's description? His accusation? " he asked.

"Haney might have lied, you know, " retorted Mr. Wynne. "Men in his position have been known to lie. "

"I understood you to say, " the chief resumed, heedless of the note of irony in the other's voice, "that you and Miss Kellner are to be married? "

"Yes. "

"And that she is the only heir of her grandfather? "

"Yes. "

"Therefore, at his death, the diamonds would become her property? "

For one instant Mr. Wynne seemed startled, and turned his clear eyes full upon his interrogator, seeking the hidden meaning.

"Yes, but—" he began slowly.

"That's true, isn't it? " demanded the chief, with quick violence.

"Yes, that's true, " Mr. Wynne admitted calmly.

"Therefore, indirectly, it would have been to your advantage if Mr. Kellner had died or had been killed? "

"In that the diamonds would have come to my intended wife, yes, " was the reply.

Mr. Czenki clasped and unclasped his thin hands nervously. His face was again expressionless, and the beady eyes were fastened immovably on Chief Arkwright's. Mr. Birnes was frankly amazed at this unexpected turn of the affair. Suddenly Chief Arkwright brought his hand down on the arm of his chair with a bang.

"Suppose, for the moment, that Red Haney lied, and that Mr. Czenki is not the murderer, then—As a matter of fact your salary isn't twenty-five thousand a year, is it? "

He was on his feet now, with blazing eyes, and one hand was thrust accusingly into Mr. Wynne's face. It was simulation; Mr. Birnes understood it; a police method of exhausting possibilities. There was not the slightest movement by Mr. Wynne to indicate uneasiness at the charge, not a tremor in his voice when he spoke again.

"I understand perfectly, Chief, " he remarked coldly. "Just what was the time of the crime, may I ask? "

"Answer my question, " insisted the Chief thunderously.

71

"Now look here, Chief, " Mr. Wynne went on frigidly, "I am not a child to be frightened into making any absurd statements. I do not draw a salary of twenty-five thousand a year, no. I am in business for myself, and make more than that. You may satisfy yourself by examining the books in my office if you like. By intimation, at least, you are accusing me of murder. Now answer me a question, please. What was the time of the crime? "

CHAPTER XV

THE TRUTH IN PART

The chief dropped back into his chair with the utmost complacency. This was not the kind of man with whom mere bluster counted.

"Haney says Saturday morning, " he answered. "The coroner's physician agrees with that. "

"Yesterday morning, " Mr. Wynne mused; then, after a moment: "I think, Chief, you know Mr. Birnes here? And that you would accept a statement of his as correct? "

"Yes, " the chief agreed with a glance at Mr. Birnes.

"Mr. Birnes, where was I all day Saturday? " Mr. Wynne queried, without so much as looking around at him.

"You were in your house from eleven o'clock Friday night until fifteen minutes of nine o'clock Saturday morning, " was the response. "You left there at that time, and took the surface car at Thirty-fourth Street to your office. You left your office at five minutes of one, took luncheon alone at the Savarin, and returned to your office at two o'clock. You remained there until five, or a few minutes past, then returned home. At eight you—"

"Is that sufficient? " interrupted Mr. Wynne. "Does that constitute an alibi? "

"Yes, " he admitted; "but how do you know all this, Birnes? "

"Mr. Birnes and the men of his agency have favored me with the most persistent attentions during the last few days, " Mr. Wynne continued promptly. "He has had two men constantly on watch at my office, day and night, and two others constantly on watch at my home, day and night. There are two there now—one in a rear room of the basement, and another in the pantry, with the doors locked on the outside. Their names are Claflin and Sutton! "

So, that was it! It came home to Mr. Birnes suddenly. Claflin and Sutton had been tricked into the house on some pretext, and locked in! Confound their stupidity!

"Why are they locked up? " demanded the chief, with kindling interest. "Why have you been watched? "

"I think, perhaps, Mr. Birnes will agree with me when I say that that has nothing whatever to do with this crime, " replied Mr. Wynne easily.

"That's for me to decide, " declared the chief bluntly.

There was a long pause. Mr. Czenki was leaning forward in his chair, gripping the arms fiercely, with his lips pressed into a thin line. It was only by a supreme effort that he held himself in control; and the lean, scarred face was working strangely.

"Well, if you insist on knowing, " observed Mr. Wynne slowly, "I suppose I'll have to tell all of it. In the first place—"

"Don't! " It came finally, the one word, from Mr. Czenki's half-closed lips, a smothered explosion which drew every eye upon him.

Mr. Wynne turned slightly in his chair and regarded the diamond expert with an expression of astonishment on his face. The beady black eyes were all aglitter with the effort of repression, and some intangible message flashed in them.

"In the first place, " resumed Mr. Wynne, as if there had been no interruption, "Mr. Kellner here—"

"Don't! " the expert burst out again desperately. "Don't! It means ruin—absolute ruin! "

"Mr. Kellner had those diamonds—about sixty thousand dollars' worth of them, " Mr. Wynne continued distinctly. "Mr. Kellner decided to sell some diamonds. One of the quickest and most satisfactory methods of selling rough gems, such as those you have in your hand, Chief, is to offer them directly to the men who deal in them. I went to Mr. Henry Latham, and other jewelers of New York, on behalf of Mr. Kellner, and offered them a quantity of diamonds. It may be that they regarded the quantity I offered as unusual; that I don't know, but I would venture the conjecture that they did. "

He paused a moment. Mr. Czenki's face, again growing expressionless, was turned toward the light of the window; Chief Arkwright was studying it shrewdly.

"Diamond merchants, of course, have to be careful, " the young man went on smoothly. "They can't afford to buy whatever is offered by people whom they don't know. They had reason, too, to believe that I was not acting for myself alone. What was more natural, therefore, than that they should have called in Mr. Birnes, and the men of his agency, to find out about me, and, if possible, to find out whom I represented, so they might locate the supply? I wouldn't tell them, because it was not desirable that they should deal directly with Mr. Kellner, who was old and childish, and lacking, perhaps, in appreciation of the real value of diamonds.

"The result of all this was that the diamond dealers placed me under strict surveillance. My house was watched; my office was watched. My mail going and coming, was subjected to scrutiny; my telephone calls were traced; telegrams opened and read. I had anticipated all this, of course, and was in communication with Mr. Kellner here only by carrier-pigeons. " He glanced meaningly at Mr. Birnes, who was utterly absorbed in the recital. "Those carrier-pigeons were not exchanged by express, because the records would have furnished a clew to Mr. Birnes' men; I personally took them back and forth in a suitcase before I approached Mr. Latham with the original proposition. "

He was giving categorical answers to a few of the multitude of questions to which Mr. Birnes had been seeking answers. The tense expression about Mr. Czenki's eyes was dissipated, and he sighed a little.

"I saw the Red Haney affair in the newspapers this morning, as you will know, " he continued after a moment. "It was desirable that I should come here with Miss Kellner, but it was not desirable, even under those circumstances, that I should permit myself to be followed. That's how it happens that Mr. Claflin and Mr. Sutton are now locked up in my house. " Again there was a pause. "Mr. Birnes, I know, will be glad to confirm my statement of the case in so far as his instructions from Mr. Latham and the other gentlemen interested bear on it? "

Chief Arkwright glanced at the detective inquiringly.

"That's right, " Mr. Birnes admitted with an uncertain nod — "that is, so far as my instructions go. I understood, though, that the diamonds were worth more than sixty thousand dollars; in fact, that there might have been a million dollars' worth of them. "

"A million dollars! " repeated Chief Arkwright in amazement. "A million dollars! " he repeated. He turned fiercely upon Mr. Wynne. "What about that? " he demanded.

"I'm sure I don't know what Mr. Birnes understood, " replied the young man, with marked emphasis. "But it's preposterous on the face of it, isn't it? Would a man with a million dollars' worth of diamonds live in a hovel like this? "

The chief considered the matter reflectively for a minute or more, the while his keen eyes alternately searched the faces of Mr. Wynne and Mr. Czenki.

"It would depend on the man, of course, " he said at last. And then some new idea was born within him. "Your direct connection with the crime seems to be disproved, Mr. Wynne, " he remarked slowly; "and if we admit his innocence, " he jerked a thumb at the expert, "there remains yet another view-point. Do you see it? "

The young man turned upon him quickly.

"Does it occur to you that every argument I advanced to furnish you with a motive for the crime might be applied with equal weight against — against Miss Kellner? "

"Doris! " flamed Mr. Wynne. For the first time his perfect self-possession deserted him, and he came to his feet with gripping hands. "Why — why — ! What are you talking about? "

"Sit down, " advised the chief quietly.

Mr. Czenki glanced at them once uneasily, then resumed his fixed stare out of the window.

"Sit down, " said the chief again.

Mr. Wynne glared at him for an instant, then dropped back into his chair. His hands were clenched desperately, and a slight flush in his clean-cut face showed the fight he was making to restrain himself.

"All the property this old man owned, including the diamonds, would become her property in the event of his death—or murder, " the chief added mercilessly. "That's true, isn't it? "

"But when she entered this room her every act testified to her innocence, " Mr. Wynne burst out passionately.

The chief shrugged his shoulders.

"She has been living at a little hotel in Irving Place, " the young man rushed on. "The people there can satisfy you as to her whereabouts on Saturday? "

Again the chief shrugged his shoulders.

"And remember, please, that the best answer to all that is that Haney had the diamonds! "

"It doesn't necessarily follow, Mr. Wynne, " said the other steadily, "that she committed the crime with her own hands. It comes down simply to this: If there were only sixty thousand dollars' worth of diamonds then the one motive which Czenki might have had is eliminated; because Haney had practically fifty thousand dollars' worth of them, and here are some others. There would have been no share for your expert here. And again, if there were only sixty thousand dollars' worth of the diamonds you or Miss Kellner would have been the only persons to benefit by this death. "

"But Haney had those! " protested Mr. Wynne.

"Just what I'm saying, " agreed the other complacently. "Therefore there were more than sixty thousand dollars' worth. However we look at it, whoever may have been Haney's accomplice, that point seems settled. "

"Or else Haney lied, " declared Mr. Wynne flatly. "If Haney came here alone, killed this old man and stole the diamonds there would be none of these questions, would there? "

Mr. Birnes, who had listened silently, arose suddenly and left the room. Mr. Wynne's last suggestion awakened a new train of thought in the police official's mind, and he considered it silently for a moment. Finally he shook his head.

"The fact remains, " he said, as if reassuring himself, "that Haney described an accomplice, that that description fits Czenki perfectly, that Czenki has refused to defend himself or even make a denial; that he has drawn suspicion upon himself by everything he has done and said since he has been here, even by the strange manner of his appearance at this house. Therefore, there were more diamonds, and he got his share of them. "

"Hello! " came in Mr. Birnes' voice from the hall. "Give me 21845 River, New York. . .. Yes. . .. Is Mr. Latham there? . .. Yes, Henry Latham . . .. "

Again Mr. Wynne's self-possession forsook him, and he came to his feet, evidently with the intention of interrupting that conversation. He started forward, with gritting teeth, and simultaneously Chief Arkwright, Detective-Sergeant Connelly and Mr. Czenki laid restraining hands upon him. Something in the expert's grip on his wrist caused him to stop and cease a futile struggle; then came a singular expression of resignation about the mouth and he sat down again.

"Hello! This Mr. Latham! . . .. This is Detective Birnes. . .. I've been able to locate some diamonds, but it's necessary to know something of the quantity of those you mentioned. You remember Mr. Schultze said something about . . .. Yes. . .. Yes. . .. Oh, there were? .. Unexpected developments, yes. . .. I'll call and see you to-night about eight. . .. Yes. . .. Good-by! "

Mr. Birnes reentered the room, his face aglow with triumph. Mr. Wynne glanced almost hopelessly at Mr. Czenki, then turned again to the detective.

"I should say there were more than sixty thousand dollars' worth of them, " Mr. Birnes blurted. "There were at least a million dollars' worth. Mr. Schultze intimated as much to me; now Mr. Latham confirms it. "

Chief Arkwright turned and glared scowlingly upon the diamond expert. The beady black eyes were alight with some emotion which he failed to read.

"Where are they, Czenki? " demanded the chief harshly.

"I have nothing to say, " replied Mr. Czenki softly.

"So your disappearance Friday night, and your absence all day yesterday did have to do with this old man's death? " said the chief, directly accusing him.

"I have nothing to say, " murmured Mr. Czenki.

"That settles it, gentlemen, " declared the chief with an air of finality. "Czenki, I charge you with the murder of Mr. Kellner here. Anything you may say will be used against you. Come along, now; don't make any trouble. "

CHAPTER XVI

MR. CZENKI EXPLAINS

Fairly drunk with excitement, his lean face, usually expressionless, now flushed and working strangely, and his beady black eyes aglitter, Mr. Czenki reeled into the study where Mr. Latham and Mr. Schultze sat awaiting Mr. Birnes. He raised one hand, enjoining silence, closed the door, locked it and placed the key in his pocket, after which he turned upon Mr. Latham.

"He makes them, man! He makes them! " he burst out between gritting teeth. "Don't you understand? He makes them! "

Mr. Latham, astonished and a little startled, came to his feet; the phlegmatic German sat still, staring at the expert without comprehension. Mr. Czenki's thin fist was clenched under his employer's nose, and the jeweler drew back a little, vaguely alarmed.

"I don't understand what—" he began.

"The diamonds! " Mr. Czenki interrupted, and the long pent-up excitement within him burst into a flame of impatience. "The diamonds! He makes them! Don't you see? Diamonds! He manufactures them! "

"Gott in Himmel! " exclaimed Mr. Schultze, and it was anything but an irreverent ejaculation. He arose. "Der miracle has come to pass! Ve might haf known! Ve might haf known! "

"Millions and millions of dollars' worth of them, even billions, for all we know, " the expert rushed on in incoherent violence. "A sum greater than all the combined wealth of the world in the hands of one man! Think of it! " Mr. Latham only gazed at him blankly, and he turned instinctively to the one who understood—Mr. Schultze. "Think of the mind that achieved it, man! "

He collapsed into a chair and sat looking at the floor, his fingers writhing within one another, muttering to himself. Mr. Latham was a cold, sane, unimaginative man of business. As yet the full import of it all hadn't reached him. He stared dumbly, first at Mr. Czenki, then at Mr. Schultze. There was not even incredulity in the look, only faint amazement that two such well-balanced men should have gone mad at once. At last the German importer turned upon him flatly.

"Why don'd you ged egzited aboud id, Laadham? " he demanded. "He iss all righd, nod crazy, " he added with whimsical assurance. "He iss delling you dat dose diamonds are made—made like doughnuds, mitoud der hole; manufactured, pud togedher. Don'd you ged id? "

He ran off into guttural German expletives; and slowly, slowly the idea began to dawn upon Mr. Latham. The diamonds Mr. Wynne had shown were not real, then; they were artificial! It was some sort of a swindle! Of course! But the experts had agreed that they were diamonds—real diamonds! Perhaps they had been deceived, or—by George! Did these two men mean to say that they were real diamonds, but that they were manufactured? Mr. Latham's tidy little imagination balked at that. Absurd! Whoever heard of a diamond as big as the Koh-i-noor, or the Regent, or the Orloff being made? They were crazy—the pair of them!

"Do I understand, " he demanded in a tone of deliberate annoyance, "that you, Czenki, and you, Schultze, expect me to believe that those diamonds we saw were not natural, but were real diamonds turned out by machinery in a—in a diamond factory? Is that what you are driving at?

"Das iss! " declared the German bluntly. "Id vas coming in dime, Laadham, id vas coming, of course Und I haf always noticed dat whatever iss coming does come. "

"Made, made—made as you make marbles, " Mr. Czenki repeated monotonously. "Yes, it had to come, but—but imagine the insuperable difficulties that one brain had to surmount! " He passed a thin hand across his flushed brow, and was thoughtfully silent.

"I don't believe it, " asserted Mr. Latham tartly. "It's impossible! I don't believe it! " And sat down.

"Id don'd madder much whedher you belief id or nod, " remarked the German in a tone of resignation. "If id iss, id iss. Und all dose diamonds in your place und mine are nod worth much more by der bushel as potatoes. "

Mr. Latham turned away from him, half angrily, and glared at the expert, who was still regarding the floor.

"What do you know about this, anyway, Czenki? " he demanded. "How do you know he makes them? Have you seen him make them? "

Thus directly addressed Mr. Czenki looked up, and the living flame of wonder within his eyes flickered and died. In silence, for a minute or more, he studied the unconcealed skepticism in his employer's face, and then asked slowly:

"Do you know what diamonds are, Mr. Latham? "

"There is some theory that they are pure carbon, crystallized. "

"They are that, " declared the expert impatiently. "You know that diamonds have been made? "

"Oh, I've read something about it, yes; but what I—"

"Every school-boy knows how to make a diamond, Mr. Latham. If pure carbon is heated to approximately five thousand degrees Fahrenheit, and simultaneously subjected to a pressure of approximately six thousand tons to the square inch, it becomes a diamond. And there's no theory about that—that's a fact! The difficulty has always been to apply the knowledge we have in a commercially practicable way—in other words, to isolate a carbon that is absolutely pure, and invent a method of applying the heat and pressure simultaneously. It has been done, Mr. Latham; it has been done! Don't you understand what it means to—"

With an effort he repressed the returning excitement which found vent in a rising voice and quick, nervous gestures of the hands. After a moment he went on:

"Half a score of scientists have made diamonds, minute particles no larger than the point of a pin. Professor Henri Moissan, of Paris, went further, and by use of an electric furnace produced diamonds as large as a pinhead. You may remember that when I first met Mr. Wynne he inquired if I had not done some special work for Professor Moissan. I had; I tested the diamonds he made—and they were diamonds! I dare say the suggestion Mr. Wynne conveyed to me by that question—that is, the suggestion of manufactured diamonds—had been carefully planned, for he is a wonderful young man, Mr. Wynne— a wonderful young man. " He paused a moment. "We know that he has millions and millions of dollars' worth of them—we know because we saw them—and who can tell how many billions more there are? The one man holds in his hand the power to overturn the money values of the earth! "

"But how do you know he makes them? " demanded Mr. Latham, returning to the main question.

"He suggested it by his question, " Mr. Czenki went on. "That suggestion lingered in my mind. When the detective, Mr. Birnes, reported that Mr. Wynne was an importer of brown sugar I was on the point of advancing a theory that the diamonds were manufactured, because of all known substances burnt brown sugar is richest in carbon. But you, Mr. Latham, had discredited a previous suggestion of mine, and I—I—well, I didn't suggest it. Instead, that night I personally began an investigation to see what disposition was made of the sugar. I found that the ships discharged their cargoes in Hoboken, that the sugar was there loaded on barges, and those barges hauled up a small stream to the little town of Coaldale, all consigned to a Mr. Hugo Kellner.

"It took Friday, all day Saturday, and a great part of to-day to learn all this. This afternoon I went to see Mr. Kellner. I found him murdered. " He stated it merely as an inconvenient incident. "In the room with the body were Mr. Birnes, Chief Arkwright of the New York police, and another New York detective. I had glanced at the story of Red Haney and the diamonds in the morning papers, and from what I knew, and from Mr. Birnes' presence, I surmised something of the truth. I was instantly placed under arrest for murder—the murder of this man I had never seen—the real diamond master, the man who achieved it all. "

He was silent for a moment, as if from infinite weariness.

" . .. Mr. Wynne came, and a Miss Kellner, granddaughter of the dead man. . .. He saw me, and understood . .. between us we contrived that I should be taken away as the murderer, and so prevent an immediate search of the house. . .. I made no denial. . .. I permitted myself to be taken . .. some mistake as to identity. . .. I proved an alibi by the shipping men in Hoboken . .. the diamonds are there, untold millions of dollars' worth of them . .. the diamond master is dead! "

Mr. Latham had been listening, as if dazed, to the hurried, somewhat disconnected, narrative; Mr. Schultze, keener to comprehend all that the story meant, was silent for a moment.

"Den if all dose men know all he has told us, Laadham, " he remarked finally, "our diamonds are nod worth any more as potatoes alretty. "

"But they don't know, " Mr. Czenki burst out fiercely. "Don't you understand? Haney, or somebody, killed Mr. Kellner and stole some uncut diamonds—you must have seen the newspaper account of it to-day. The New York police traced Haney's course to Coaldale and to that house. But all they know is that sixty thousand dollars' worth of uncut stones were stolen. There was not even a suggestion to them of the millions and millions of dollars' worth that were manufactured. Don't you understand? I permitted myself to be accused and arrested, knowing I could establish an alibi, in order to lead them away from there and gain time, at least, to give Mr. Wynne an opportunity of hiding the other diamonds, if they were there. He understood what I was trying to do, and fell in with the plan. He knew that I knew the diamonds were made. Mr. Birnes doesn't know; no one knows but you and me and Mr. Wynne, and perhaps the girl! But, don't you see, if you don't accept the proposition he made the diamond market of the world is ruined? You are ruined! "

"But how do you know they are made? " insisted Mr. Latham doggedly. "You've never seen them made, have you? "

"Mein Gott, Laadham, how do you know when you haf der boil on der pack of your neck? You can'd zee him, ain'd id? " Mr. Schultze turned to Mr. Czenki. "Der dhree of us vill go und zee Mr. Wynne. Id iss der miracle! Vass iss, iss, und id don'd do any good to say id ain'd. "

CHAPTER XVII

THE GREAT CUBE

A cube of solid, polished steel, some twenty feet square, set on a spreading base of concrete, and divided perpendicularly down the middle into Titanic halves, these being snugly fitted one to the other by a series of triangular corrugations, a variation of the familiar tongue and groove. Interlacing the ponderous mass, from corner to corner, were huge steel bolts, and the hulking heads of more bolts, some forty on each of the four sides, showed that the whole might be split into halves at will, and readily made whole again, one enormous side sliding back and forth on a short track.

In the two undivided faces of the cube, relatively squaring the center, were four borings somewhat smaller in diameter than an ordinary pencil, and extending through; and directly in the center was focused a network of insulated wires which dropped down out of the gloom overhead. In the other two sides of the great cube, just where the dividing lines of the halves came, were the funnel-like mouths of a two-inch boring. This, too, extended straight through.

Directly opposite each of the two mouths, a dozen feet away, was mounted a peculiarly-constructed heavy gun of the naval type. In a general sort of way these were not unlike twelve-inch ordnance, but the breech was much larger in proportion, the barrel longer, and the bore only two instead of twelve inches. The mountings were high, and the adjustment so delicate that, looking into the open breech of one gun, the bore through the twenty-foot cube and through the barrel of the gun on the other side seemed to be continuous.

"This is the diamond-making machine, gentlemen, " said Mr. Wynne, and he indicated to Mr. Latham, Mr. Schultze and Mr. Czenki the cube and the two guns. "It is perfectly simple in construction, has enormous powers of resistance, as you may guess, and is as delicately fitted as a watch, being regulated by electric power. This cube is the solution of the high-pressure, high-temperature problem, which was only one of the many seemingly insuperable obstacles to be overcome. When the bolts are withdrawn one half slides back; when the bolts are in position it is as solid as if it were in one piece, and perfectly able to withstand a force greater than the ingenuity of man has ever before been able to contrive. This force is a combination of a heat one-half that of the sun on its surface, and a head-on impact of two one-hundred-pound projectiles fired less than forty feet apart with an enormous charge of cordite, and possessing an initial velocity greater than was ever recorded in gunnery.

"This vast force centers in a sort of furnace in the middle of the cube. The furnace is round, about three feet long and three feet in diameter, built of half a dozen fire-resisting substances in layers, perforated for electric wires, with an opening through it lengthwise of the exact size of the borings in the guns and in the cube. It fits snugly into a receptacle cut out for it in the center of the cube, and is intended to protect the steel of the cube proper from the intense heat. This heat reaches the furnace by electric wires which enter the cube from the sides, as you see, being brought here by a conduit along the river-bed from a large power-plant five miles away. Twenty-eight large wires are necessary to bring it; I own the power-plant, ostensibly for the operation of a small sugar refinery. I may add that the furnace is a variation of the principle employed by Professor Moissan, in Paris. " He turned to Mr. Czenki. "You may remember having heard me mention him? "

"I remember, " the expert acquiesced grimly.

"Now, pure carbon is vaporized, as you perhaps know, at a fraction less than five thousand degrees Fahrenheit, " Mr. Wynne continued. "A carbon not merely chemically pure but absolutely pure, in highly compressed disks, is packed in the furnace, the furnace placed within the cube, the ends of the two-inch opening in the furnace being blocked to prevent expansion, the cube closed, the bolts fastened, and heat applied, for several minutes—a heat, gentlemen, of five thousand two hundred and eighty degrees Fahrenheit. The heat of the sun is only about ten thousand degrees. And then the pressure of about seven thousand tons to the square inch is added by means of the two guns. In other words, gentlemen, pure carbon, vaporized, is caught between two projectiles which enter the cube simultaneously from opposite sides, being fired by electricity. The impact is so terrific that what had been two feet of compressed carbon is instantly condensed into an irregular disk, one inch or an inch and a half thick. And that disk, gentlemen, is a diamond!

"The violence of the operation, coupled with the intense heat, fuses everything—furnace, projectiles, electric wires, fire-brick, even asbestos, into a single mass. The cube is opened, and this mass, white-hot, is dropped into cold water. This increases the pressure until the mass is cool. Then it is broken away, and in the center is a diamond—as big as a biscuit, gentlemen! Four small bores lead from the two-inch bore through the cube, and permit the escape of air as the projectiles enter. There is no rebound because the elastic quality of the carbon is crushed out of existence—driven, I may say, into the diamond itself. Of course the furnace, the two projectiles and the connecting electric wires are all destroyed at each charge, which brings the total cost of the operation to a little more than eight hundred dollars, including nearly three tons of brown sugar. The diamond resulting is worth at least a million when broken up for cutting, sometimes even two millions. That is all, I think. "

There was a long, awed silence. Mr. Latham, leaning against the giant cube, stared thoughtfully at his toes; Mr. Schultze was peering curiously about him, thence off into the gloom; Mr. Czenki still had a question.

"I understand that all the diamonds were made in that disk-like shape, " he remarked at last. "Then the uncut stones that were stolen were—"

"They were natural stones, " interrupted Mr. Wynne, "imported for purposes of study and experiment. I told Chief Arkwright the truth, but not all of it. In the last twenty years Mr. Kellner had destroyed some twenty thousand dollars' worth of diamonds in this way. I may add that while Mr. Kellner had succeeded in making diamonds of large size he had never made a perfect one until eight years ago. But meanwhile the expenses of the work, as you will understand, were enormous, so during the past eight years about a million dollars' worth of diamonds have been sold, one or two at a time, to meet this expense. "

He paused a moment, then resumed musingly:

"All this, you understand, is not the work of a day Mr. Kellner was nearly eighty-one years old, and it was fifty-eight years ago that he began work here. The cubes there were made and placed in position thirty years ago; the guns have been there for twenty-eight years— so long, in fact, that recollection of them has passed from the minds of the men who made them. And, until four years ago, he was assisted by his son, Miss Kellner's father, and her brother. There was some explosion in this chamber where we stand which killed them both, and since then he has worked alone. His son—Miss Kellner's father—was the inventor of the machine which has enabled us to cut all the stones I showed you. I mailed the application for patent on this machine to Washington three days ago. It is as intricate as a linotype and delicate as a chronometer, but it does the work of fifty expert hand-cutters. Until patent papers are granted I must ask that I be allowed to protect that. "

Mr. Latham turned upon him quickly.

"But you've explained all this to us fully, " he exclaimed sharply, indicating the cube and the guns. "We could duplicate that if we liked. "

"Yes, you could, Mr. Latham, " replied Mr. Wynne slowly, "but you can't duplicate the brain that isolated absolutely pure carbon from the charred residue of brown sugar. That brain was Mr. Kellner's; the secret died with him! "

Again there was a long silence, broken at last by Mr. Schultze:

"Dat means no more diamonds can be made undil some one else can make der pure carbon, ain'd id? Yah! Und dat brings us down to der question, How many diamonds are made alretty? "

"The diamonds I showed you gentlemen were all that have been cut thus far, " replied Mr. Wynne. "Less than twenty of the disks were used in making them. There are now some five hundred more of these disks in existence—roughly a billion dollars' worth—so you see I am prepared to hold you to my proposition that you buy one hundred million dollars' worth of them at one-half the carat price you now pay in the open market. "

Mr. Latham passed one hand across a brow bedewed with perspiration, and stared helplessly at the German.

"The work of cutting could go on steadily here, under the direction of Mr. Czenki, " Mr. Wynne resumed after a moment. "The secrecy of this place has not been violated for forty years. We are now one hundred and seventy feet below ground level, in a gallery of the abandoned coal mine which gave Coaldale its name, reached underground from the cellar in the cottage. Roofs and walls of the entire place are shored up to insure safety, and heavy felts make this chamber sound-proof, smothering even the detonation of the guns. Mr. Czenki is the man to do the work. Mr. Kellner, for ten years, held him to be the first expert in the world, and it would be carrying out his wishes if Mr. Czenki would agree. If he does not I shall undertake it, and flood the market! " His voice hardened a little. "And, gentlemen, call off your detectives. The secret is now more yours than mine. It destroys you if it becomes known, not me! The New York police have turned this end of the investigation over to the local police, and they are fools; all the forms have been complied with, so this place is safe. Now call off your men! On the day the last diamond is delivered to you, and the payment of one hundred million dollars is completed, everything here will be destroyed. That's all! "

"One hundred million dollars! " repeated Mr. Latham. "Even if we accept the proposition, Schultze, how can we raise that enormous sum within a year, and preserve the secret? "

"Id ain'd a question of can, Laadham—id's a question of musd, " was the reply. He thoughtfully regarded Mr. Wynne. "Id's only Sunday nighd, yed; we haf undil Thursday to answer, you remember. " He turned to Mr. Latham, with a recurrence of whimsical philosophy. "Think of id, Laadham, der alchemisds tried for dhree thousand years to make a piece of gold so big as a needle-point und didn'd; und he made diamonds so big as your fist mit a liddle cordide und some elecdricity! Mein Gott, man! Think of id! "

The jewelers accepted Mr. Wynne's proposition. Mr. Wynne bowed his thanks, and handed to Mr. Czenki a scientific periodical opened at a page which bore a head-line:

> Newly Discovered Property of Radium.
> Diamonds, Rubies, Emeralds and Sapphires
> Changed in Color by Exposure of One
> Month to Radium.

For the fourth time Red Haney underwent the "third degree. " It culminated in a full confession of the murder of Mr. Kellner. There had been no accomplice.

"Yer see, Chief, " he explained apologetically, "you an' that other guy" (meaning Mr. Birnes) "was so dead set on sayin' there was somebody else in it, an' was so ready wit' yer descriptions, that it looked good to me, an' I said 'Sure, ' but I done it. "

Lightning Source UK Ltd.
Milton Keynes UK
UKHW011834270121
377760UK00001B/41

9 781406 581164